Cecil
&
Noreen

Patrick Corcoran

seren

Seren is the book imprint of
Poetry Wales Press Ltd
Nolton Street, Bridgend, CF31 3BN, Wales
www.seren-books.com.

© Patrick Corcoran, 2005

ISBN 1-85411-388-7

The author wishes to acknowledge the award
of a bursary from the Arts Council of Wales
for the purpose of writing this book.

The publisher works with the financial assistance of the
Welsh Books Council.

Printed in Plantin by Bell & Bain Ltd, Glasgow.

Cecil
&
Noreen

For Bim, Anna and Liz

January, 1999

IT SOUNDS BORING, if one considers only the words Noreen utters – "I first met Cecil in church, you know". As churches go, the Catholic church in Chard was neither more nor less dull than a dozen or so other Catholic churches in which Noreen has worshipped up until now. She has been in so many during her lifetime, she hardly notices anything about them anymore – apart from how cold or well-heated they are.

When Noreen says she first met Cecil in church, however, it sounds exciting, intense, like a chance encounter during a hazardous jungle expedition when each was running low on supplies, he lacking water and she food, and she somehow makes it seem as if their meeting at that particular moment in their very separate lives was not only a fortuitous accident but their very salvation, neither having ever again to face the world alone, no matter how obtuse the other was, how their natures diverged or how opposed one was to the opinion of the other. She throws back her head and goes into gales of laughter as she describes how she accidentally struck Cecil on the back of his head with a religious banner dedicated to Our Lady, which she was carrying in a procession.

At the time when Noreen and Cecil met, she was teaching at the local convent school. Living in with the nuns. Saint Gildas' Convent School, Chard. That sounds boring too, a young woman of 22 living in a convent. But Noreen did not feel boring. On the contrary, she felt great surges of life coursing through her veins.

Noreen recalls details of the procession as if it was yesterday. Because she was at the front of The Children of

7

Mary carrying the banner, she was following the back end of The Knights Of Saint Columba who were progressing in a dignified fashion ahead of herself and the group of girls from the convent school who constituted The Children Of Mary. Noreen says she had already noticed a tall young man with a particularly fine head and proud bearing, in front of her. Almost noble in appearance, she thought. What she could see was the rear view of a short-back-and-sides haircut, the back of a crisp tweed jacket, with its smart vent in the middle, on a ram-rod straight back, fawn cavalry twill trousers, and well-polished heels on sensible brown shoes.

The thing that impressed Noreen most, however, was the intensity of Cecil's devotion to the object of the procession. His almost quivering concentration on the task in hand. Not for him, staring vaguely at the rafters wondering what he would be having for tea, like some of the other men. His head was bowed at an angle which would have caused any ordinary mortal a seriously damaged neck, and each foot was placed so carefully and devoutly in front of the other that every muscle in his slight frame must have ached as it complied with Cecil's demand for rigorous self-control. After she had struck Cecil to the ground with Our Lady's banner – "How else was I to see what he looked like from the front?" she asks innocently – Noreen was able to register his high forehead and this confirmed her opinion that he was intelligent and of very handsome appearance; his black hair brushed straight back in a no-nonsense style; the wire-rimmed spectacles reflecting the church lights above him as he lay supine beneath her, gasping for breath; the gingery moustache bristling like hog's hair, – that will have to go, she thought immediately, but it never did; the firm chin, almost stubborn, sticking out just that bit too far; and the eyes, brown, soft, vulnerable. As she looked into those eyes, she experienced a sense of falling in, drowning in them. It was not the eyes themselves, appealing though they were to her, and she decides she cannot even now convey adequately to others the immediate effect that his eyes had upon her, it was that she felt here was someone who had a need for something, for someone, for her. She felt she had stumbled upon part of herself which she had no idea she had lost somewhere along the way of her life thus far, as if in finding Cecil she had found a twin whom she had not known existed, a non-identical twin, but a twin nonetheless.

Gently pressed, Noreen paints the picture a little more fully. They met on a day in May. The month devoted to Our Lady. There were always processions in Our Lady's honour on Sunday afternoons. First, they would process down the main aisle and around the church, then outside into the fresh Somerset air, and finally three times around the Church grounds before re-entering the church. It brought a bit of life to the service, going outside where the wind often played havoc with the priest's robes, the banners and the altar boys' candles.

The banner which Noreen was carrying was large and heavy. It was supported on a mahogany pole, with a mahogany cross-piece to which an embroidered tapestry was attached with canvas loops. It was her first time carrying the banner. A nun from the convent, Sister Immaculata, who had previously done it from time immemorial, had become too old. How she had managed it at all was a source of great wonder to Noreen, when she first supported the banner's weight.

As Noreen was processing down the main aisle towards the porch, she noticed at the last moment that, to pass beneath the choir stalls without hitting them, she would need to lower her banner. She tipped it forwards quickly and the weight of the banner did the rest. Cecil was smitten and he fell, or rather crumpled in a heap on the wooden tiles, ending up on his back but with his legs continuing to step piously in mid air, as if unaware of the bolt which had struck their owner out of the blue.

"Oh dear, oh dear... I'm so sorry." Before Cecil had time to wonder what had happened to him, in the merest blink of an eye, Noreen was above him and had arrived in his life, whether he liked it or not.

"I'm really sorry." Even as her gaze became conjoined with Cecil's, having established that he had not been knocked permanently senseless, Noreen could not help laughing out loud at what had happened.

"I am sorry, really... It was an accident."

"That's quite all right," Cecil said, as if quite glad to have had the back of his cranium struck with considerable force, for no other reason than that he had been taking part in a procession in honour of Our Lady and walking in front of Noreen.

CECIL SEEMS TO BE DROWSING, nodding his head in time to the drumming of his fingers on the bedside locker. His eyes are closed but he cannot be asleep. It would be impossible to drum his fingers on the bedside locker, if he were asleep. He begins to speak very quietly, but it is just possible to make out words, and his determination to express himself is apparent in the immense effort he makes to clearly enunciate every syllable. He wonders whether perhaps he might be allowed to say something now, if Noreen has quite finished for the moment. It is possible to discern a slight note of irritation in Cecil's tone today over the fact that Noreen has held the floor so long. He says he does seem to remember that it was in Chard they met. That Chard is where "that happy event took place", is how he puts it. He says he can remember it all perfectly. He can even remember what he was thinking about just before the banner hit him on the back of the head. He will not tell Noreen what it was though. It was something about The Knights Of Saint Columba is all he will say. A confidential matter.

Before he and Noreen met, Cecil had more or less resigned himself to continuing in his position as a postal clerk in the Chard Post Office and spending most of his leisure hours participating in church activities, organising whist drives, Christmas Fayres, and doing good works with The Knights Of Saint Columba and other worthy organisations. At the end of a typically busy day, he sometimes nurtured the hope that someone suitable would come his way, though less and less often had that possibility passed through his mind as time went on.

He was still living at home and had reached the stage where he no longer even felt embarrassed when his mother called him 'Twas', short for 'Twasles', his nick-name, finding that this appellation created a reassuring sense of security in him which he had not yet been able to experience in any other way.

He often thought about The Knights Of Saint Columba, for want of anything more romantic to divert him. The Knights called each other 'brother' and took a vow to keep their society's business secret. In all probability, Noreen guesses, he had been thinking about the likely cost of hiring a local hall, perhaps to run a beetle drive to raise funds for the poor families of the parish. In any event, he clearly remembers being suddenly distracted from his thoughts, whatever they were about, by a sudden blow to the back of his head. On regaining consciousness a few seconds later, he felt convinced that something important had happened, but realised later that may simply have been as a result of the blow to his head. He vividly remembers lying stretched out on the church floor then looking up into Noreen's face, and has associated the smell of good floor polish with Noreen's face ever since, especially when she looks at him from above, laughing. He says he can still picture that young woman's face which stared so closely into his, saying repeatedly she was so sorry between irrepressible bouts of laughter. A face which has changed little, he adds gallantly.

He sternly disapproved of Noreen laughing in church, he says, frowning playfully, but that disapproval soon changed to joy when they met up for a cup of tea in the church hall after the service and discovered that they shared a passion for history and church architecture which led them to embark on many fascinating trips together.

His abiding memory is of surprise, on this day when his life changed, he says. Of being so stunned that, as he looked up and saw Noreen's hair framing her face, glowing brightly in the light from the lamp in the church roof above and behind her, he was not sure where he was. He wondered whether he was already amongst the heavenly hosts until Noreen started apologising and laughing, and then a bit of a headache came on and he knew he was still on earth.

CECIL IS A MAN OF FEW WORDS. You have to catch him on a good day, if you want him to talk. When he is out in his wheelchair he gets tired more quickly and soon begins to slump sideways if he talks for too long. Then it is a hard job to get him upright again. On good days, if he can get his chair positioned with his back to the window where he can see who is coming in and out of his room, and where he therefore feels comparatively safe, he relaxes. There is a woman who brings her dog in because she finds it cheers a lot of people up. When she comes in, Cecil pretends he cannot talk or see, because he is terrified of dogs. Noreen says to him, "Why don't you turn around so you can enjoy the view, Cecil? Look – you can see right across the roof-tops to Penarth Head. And the grounds here are beautiful – those enormous trees, they must be at least a hundred years old, magnificent, even if they don't have any leaves on them at this time of year."

Cecil simply checks again that his wheels are in line with the pattern in the carpet and stares into space until everyone settles down. He thinks a lot about his early life now, and occasionally talks as if people who have gone are still in the land of the living. It is understandable. Noreen visits for several hours twice a day, but there are inevitably long hours when he is alone. He sometimes tells his son, Sean, that Sean's grandparents, Pop and Mammy Connolly, have been in, though they have been dead for years. Says they'll be along later. Tells him they are staying here, in the same hotel. He asks Sean if he is staying, too. Sometimes he worries he is late for a meeting. Wheels himself to the lounge, where the other residents look at him blankly, and he cannot understand what has gone wrong. There are always staff around, but Cecil finds it hard to get to know them. They keep changing shifts and all wear the same white coats. It is hard to begin afresh with new people at his age.

When Cecil reminisces, he often declares that his mother was born in Chester, that he was born in Market Drayton in Shropshire, and that he is proud to be English. He recites how they lived at 49, Grosvenor Terrace, Market Drayton, until he was one year old, using words he has repeated time and again throughout his life. His father worked in the Post Office there. He often talks about Pop Connolly fighting in the British Army at The Battle of The Somme but does not advertise the fact that his father was Irish. From County Carlow. From "a village with a Gaelic name of some sort", he says dismissively. Then he tells how they moved to Tintagel in Cornwall when he was a bit older, and later on his father was made the Postmaster in Chard, where they lived when Cecil went to school, firstly at the Junior School in Chard and then Ilminster Grammar School. Again, he seems proud of the fact that he can still remember the address they lived at there – 24, Furnham Road, Chard.

Cecil's first memory of his father is of seeing him come home waving a pound note excitedly. He was very red in his face and had been drinking gin. A friend at the Post Office used to place bets for him.

"China Slipper came in first, Mammy." Pop Connolly always called Cecil's mother Mammy, which made Cecil feel jealous. She was his Mammy.

Mammy had been soaping Cecil in the little bath in front of the coal fire when Pop came bursting in. Cecil sensed, rather than saw, his mother's look as she glared at her husband, now sprawled legs akimbo in one of their sagging armchairs, searching through his pockets for his Woodbines.

"What would they think... at the Post Office? If they only knew."

"Wha'?" Pop looks at her wide-eyed, crestfallen.

Cecil suspected there was something inherently evil about alcohol and gambling for the rest of his life. According to Noreen, he only got drunk once in his life – on their honeymoon during the war, drinking farm-house cider.

As a child, Cecil learned to spend his time doing useful things. Mammy did not like him getting his clothes muddied playing football and other rough games with children from the town. Truth to tell he did not much enjoy mixing with the neighbourhood children in any case, so he was overjoyed when Mammy told him she would try to persuade his father to buy him The Handyman's Box of Tools for his twelfth birthday. It was not inexpensive. Fifty shillings. Pop Connolly could buy a lot of gin as well as a reserve store of Jameson's whisky for that amount. She said she would ask Pop about it when he was in a good mood. Next time he had a win on the horses, she suggested it. Cecil sat quietly on a chair in the corner, judging it best to leave things to Mammy.

"Wha'..?" said Pop, when Mammy explained it would only cost fifty shillings, with carriage two and sixpence extra. It had clearly never occurred to Pop to buy such a present for Cecil. A pair of boxing gloves, or a toboggan to use in the snow – great fun – were the sort of gift he would have favoured.

"It'll be really useful," Mammy persisted quickly. "Twasles will be able to make such nice things for the house."

"Right y'are. Lucky, you mentioning it when I've had a bit o' luck with the horses. Go ahead – get the boy what he wants for his birthday."

Although it had been Mammy's idea, Cecil wrote

delightedly in his diary for that year a list of every tool which the box contained.

Yippee! I've now got a claw hammer, a number ten plane, four inch screwdriver, bradawl, ten inch handsaw, keyhole saw, half inch chisel, half inch gouge, steel rule, marking gauge, number one registered vice, nine inch tenon saw, small spokeshave, box of nails, a sandpaper block, glue pot, ten inch mitre block, steel square, and an illustrated hand book of instructions and working drawings. All I've got to do now is learn how to use them!

He still has the diary in his bedside locker, somehow squashed in with a multitude of other private papers.

During his thirteenth year, he pestered Mammy until she agreed to stump up tuppence a week for *Hobbies, The Fretworker's Weekly For All Amateurs & Craftsmen*. This became Cecil's bible and was his favourite reading each evening after he had finished his homework. He turned out many small masterpieces, including two photograph frames into which he placed a picture of Pop Connolly in his army uniform and one of Mammy taken in a photographer's studio. Before his thirteenth birthday he surpassed himself and made A Small Sideboard For the Living Room. He managed it with the basic handyman's tools at his disposal, even though the design incorporated a technically difficult love-heart motif in the two top corners.

"There we are. This is for the two of you," Cecil said when it was finished and he brought it in from the shed where he had been labouring on it in secret. He lowered it to the ground in the living room.

"Twas!..." was all Mammy could say, as she clasped him tightly to her, against the slightly faded floral apron she was wearing at the time, having just finished washing up the tea things in the kitchen. It smelt of starch and fresh air and butter all at once and Cecil could not have been prouder of himself at that moment.

"Well, I'll go to F-F-F-Fishponds..." Pop said, reaching into his pocket for a shilling which he slipped into Cecil's hand whilst Cecil was still half-suffocating in Mammy's bony bosom.

The sideboard was moved into the tiny front parlour immediately, it being felt that only the best room was worthy of housing it. There was not a lot of floor space left when it was installed there but Mammy moved out a little nest of tables to make room and transferred a porcelain mandolin player, which had belonged to her mother and had been standing on one of the tables, to its new special place on the top shelf of the sideboard.

Buoyed up by this success, for his thirteenth birthday Cecil asked for an A1 Fret Machine which he had seen advertised in *Hobbies* magazine.

"It's a lot of money," he admitted. "55 shillings..." Out of the corner of his eye, he could see Pop Connolly's face going puce. Perhaps he had not chosen the right moment. "But it comes with a spanner, a drill bit, a dozen saws..."

"Your Pop and I will discuss it this evening," Mammy said, just in time.

"...and it's sent carriage forward to the nearest railway station, in a crate, ready for use." Cecil could not resist completing his prepared request, with all the arguments in its favour.

"Wha'... You... and where, in God's name, will I get 55 shillings from?"

"Homework, Cecil... and stay in your room." It was the first time Cecil had experienced Mammy being stern with him.

"You will not take God's name in vain, in this house, Connolly. Apologise – now!" Cecil heard the low tone of his mother's voice, as he ascended the stairs. And his father's muted tones backing down, in the face of Mammy's wrath. Cecil tried to forget it and concentrated on his English Grammar.

The next morning, after Pop had already left for the Post Office, Mammy told Cecil they had agreed that he could have a fret machine for his birthday. Cecil was delighted and managed not to mention how desperately he wanted a Hobbies Folding Bench – only sixty shillings for the four foot model – 'strong, practical, well-made'. That would have to wait until his fourteenth birthday.

When he got the fret machine out of its crate, the first thing Cecil made was an ingenious cigarette box for Pop. Cigarettes and matches went into separate compartments in the top and, when you pulled out a shallow drawer at the bottom, one cigarette and one match were ready for use. Using intricate fretwork, the legend 'Cigarettes and Matches' was tacked to the lid of the box.

"Well, I'll go to F... Have you seen what he's made now?" Pop said, when Cecil gave him the box, and he filled it with the packet of Woodbines he had in his pocket and a few Swan Vestas matches which were lying loose on the mantlepiece. The box worked like a dream. The only problem was it encouraged Pop to smoke indoors, especially when they had visitors and he was tempted to show his box off, despite knowing Mammy liked him to take a chair into the back garden when he wanted to smoke.

"It makes your clothes smell, Pop," she used to say. "And who has to wash them?..."

For Mammy, Cecil made a ukulele. The pattern for the ukulele was the closest thing to a mandolin which Cecil could find in *Hobbies* magazine. It was perfect in every respect. Even the pegs which enabled it to be properly tuned worked as they should.

"Cecil, that's beautiful," Mammy said, through her

tears. "It's a lovely tribute to my mother, isn't it? How thoughtful of you."

"I'm glad you like it," Cecil said.

Cecil's world was complete. He had his parents. His bedroom. The shed. His schoolwork. Admittedly, school itself was not much fun. Some of the other pupils, especially the boys, made fun of the fact that he was always so clean and tidy. But he felt safe in the knowledge that in the evenings he would be going home for tea with creamy milk, hot tea out of the white china teapot with the roses design, the teapot with the curvy handle fashioned in three sections, from separate pieces of clay. He liked the act of putting teaspoonsful of shiny white granulated sugar onto his spoon. Letting his spoon hover on the surface, allowing the tea to soak into the sugar and turn it brown, before tipping it into the tea as a gooey brown mixture.

He could be an alchemist, a wizard, a magician, whilst his parents talked above him about the affairs of the day. He heard what they said but was not encouraged to participate. He kept busy chasing any floating tea-leaves which the sugar had not succeeded in dragging down with it and which had evaded the china tea-strainer which Mammy meticulously placed over every cup before pouring. While they talked, he spread butter on his bread, fat creamy butter with a sheen like the sea has when it is calm and oily smooth, as it had been sometimes when they lived in Tintagel. The giant strawberries could be placed strategically, like a row of houses, on each half of the slice which he tried to cut with total precision so that neither slice was bigger than the other. Then he would take the left slice first, with his left hand as he had been taught, followed by the right slice which he would also have to pick up with his left hand. To even things up, he always ate two slices of Mammy's delicious sponge cake afterwards using his right hand, with his second cup of tea.

After his homework was done, Cecil could relax. Could look ahead to the rest of the evening, going through his magazines, when it was too dark to make anything in the garden shed. His collection of magazines was building up and he never tired of reading and re-reading the articles. They covered such a wide range – indoor winter photography, how to hide valuables from burglars by hollowing out the centre pages of any large book of no great value, information about the rules of hockey – worlds he would never have had access to without *Hobbies* magazine.

Cecil's fretwork helped him to see that order and hard work made for perfection of form. He began to try to apply this way of thinking to the world about him. Much of what he saw reflected a pattern. The emergence and re-emergence of life, contrasted with death in a cyclical fashion. Growth and decay were visible in the world around him. But people died and nobody seemed to know where they went. One day, Cecil acknowledged to himself that he was as far away from understanding it all as he had been from building a sideboard before he had any tools. His father was a Catholic but had not been to church since he was a young man in Ireland. Mammy was a member of The Church of England but had not been to any services since she and Pop Connolly married in Chester Cathedral.

Cecil remembered Pop Connolly once telling him that the Catholic Church claimed to be the one, true church. He could not understand why, if this was the case, Pop Connolly avoided Churches like the plague. He decided to have a talk with the local Catholic Parish Priest, Father Mortlake. Cecil liked the certainty of the message the priest gave him. He was told that, as long as he attended weekly Mass and kept the other rules, he would be in 'a state of grace'. He would be able to look forward to going to heaven, when he died, where he would be able to see again all the people whom he had known in life – in a state of perpetual happiness. This prospect enthralled him, as did the the injunction to 'love thy neighbour'. Cecil thought of the bullies he had to rub shoulders with at school. It was right, he thought. People should love each other, be kind to each other. At the age of fourteen and a half, Cecil was baptised. And became the most devout member of the local congregation that the parish priest had ever encountered. In due course, Cecil framed his Baptismal Certificate and, although not as ornate as the Certificate of Merit, First Class Award, from the Editor of *Hobbies*, received for 'Efficiency in Fretwork Competition', his Baptismal Certificate was a significant reminder to him of the measurable progress he had made in understanding the mystery of life.

NOREEN SAYS her earliest memory is of being born. Her parents were Jack and Kitty Byrne. Jack from Baltinglass, County Wicklow. Kitty from Ellesmere, Shropshire.

Jack was the eldest of his parents' six sons and would have inherited the family farm had he not decided to make his own way in the world. For some reason which Noreen never discovered, he decided to seek his fortune in Rhosllanerchrugog, where Noreen was born, and he worked in The Maypole grocery stores in nearby Wrexham, where he eventually became the manager. Noreen still has the gold watch they presented him with when he retired: 'J. Byrne from MAYPOLE for loyal service 1907-1955' – 48 years devotion to duty, prime cuts of bacon and the housewives of the town of Wrexham. Whenever Noreen visited Wrexham with her father, she remembers their progress was halted every five yards or so as Jack stopped in his tracks, doffed his brown trilby and greeted one shopping-laden woman after another – "Good morning, Missus... errh" – another bustles by – "Ah, good morning, Missus... errh". "Have you met my little daughter, Missus... errh.. Noreen's her name. Isn't she a pretty one?" For years Noreen thought all the women in Wrexham were called Missus Errh, but later she understood it was her father's way of preserving a professional distance, and he knew all their names perfectly well.

Kitty, Noreen's mother, was the middle child of her parents' seven children and the eldest daughter. She left school at fourteen to learn the trade of dressmaking. She helped her mother make-do and mend, maintaining the clothes of all the other children. But the mists over the local ponds and meres bred dreams in Kitty's soul. While she hand-stitched collars with yards of thread, or lost herself in the rhythm of her sewing machine's treadle, Kitty dreamed of romantic voyages to places like India and Japan where she would concoct glittering dresses from beautiful silks and rich fabrics and meet exotic princes whose white horses roamed wild and free throughout their extensive lands.

The furthest Kitty eventually travelled from Ellesmere and Rhosllanerchrugog and their environs was when the Maypole presented Jack with his gold watch in a London hotel, and during annual holidays to far-off Aberystwyth. Kitty's Indian prince became Jack Byrne, whom she met at a jumble sale in Wrexham, where he was buying a best suit and she was looking for trousers for her youngest brother. She overheard an unusual accent and, when she spotted Jack, she liked his courteous manner as he spoke to the woman who was in charge of the men's clothes stall – "How much for this pin-striped one here?... Missus... errh?"

Jack and Kitty married in Ellesmere, set up home in a rented house in Rhosllanerchrugog, and very soon afterwards their union was blessed when Kitty became pregnant and Noreen subsequently came into the world, approximately nine months and ten days after Kitty conceived.

Although Noreen's earliest memory is of being born, there is some doubt as to whether she remembers the event proper or whether she has listened to accounts of it so frequently and from such an early age that she thinks she remembers it. Kitty's recall of Noreen's birth was indisputably vivid and dramatic – she was after all the one giving birth – it certainly seems to have been a traumatic experience for her, the memory of which has not diminished in intensity at any stage of Kitty's life. As to how exactly the confinement progressed, it is hard to glean a rational picture as, according to Noreen, whenever her birth was mentioned, Kitty used to screw up her eyes, breathlessly clutch her throat and say almost accusingly to Noreen, "I nearly died giving birth to you, you know!"

"Yes, I know. I remember." Noreen used to say, as if remembering somehow defused the fearful power of her mother's statement. Not that she had wished or willed her mother to nearly die giving birth to her, nor did she know what it had felt like, but she knew about it from her own account, her own knowledge, not her mother's.

"You were so big – nine pounds twelve ounces... very big for a girl!"

To this, Noreen had no answer. She was slightly bigger than average but tried not to feel unfeminine or clumsy. Despite herself, there were times when she felt the odd one out. Her reaction was to join in with extra energy, to push herself forward so that the experience of getting involved over-rode any latent sense of exclusion.

Noreen's mother's love of beautiful dresses and colourful fabrics came most powerfully to the fore once Noreen was born. Silk dresses bedecked with ribbons, aristocratic cloaks, lace collars, nightdresses like ball gowns – all were created for Noreen by Kitty's inspired, loving hands, throughout Noreen's childhood. Noreen felt uncomfortable about the clothes, feeling they drew attention to her excessive size, and reflected aspirations above her station in life. Luckily, being bigger than average, other girls rarely tried to bully her.

So, Noreen's memory of her birth was that she herself was lucky to be alive at all. If her mother had nearly died, a fully grown woman, how much more dangerous had it been for her, a tiny defenceless baby? She had her own picture of a wise old midwife attending her mother, washing her, calming her, bringing her back from the brink of death. She saw herself small and pink, even if bigger than average, lying on a luxuriously soft white towel. And she had a vague recollection that her father, Jack, had earlier been sitting calmly in the back garden of their little terraced house in Rhosllanerchrugog, tamping whorls of Saint Bruno's tobacco into the bowl of his pipe with his thumb before puffing away contentedly and concentrating on his potato plants, as Noreen emerged through her mother's screams of pain, and that later he had sat beside Kitty as she still lay prostrate in bed, holding a damp cloth against her temples.

It was not until Noreen was in her teens that she began to speculate as to why she remained an only child. For years she had longed for a younger sister. She had imagined herself playing such happy games with Netty. The name of her imagined sister had come to her one day when she was at the park pond with her little net, catching lots of green weed but no minnows. Noreen and Netty, she thought, went well together.

She had uncles and aunties by the dozen, and cousins by the score, most of whom had brothers or sisters. Why had she none? Kitty, who was a regular church-goer, told Noreen it was all in God's hands and human beings had to accept His will. Yet she held out some hope by adding that nobody knew what God may deign to bring to pass in the fullness of time. For that reason, Noreen was in her early twenties before she began to wonder whether the fact that she was an only child might not be pure chance.

As her parent's only child, Noreen did not have to compete with other children to become the centre of attention at home. Going to school was always going to be a shock to her system, even going to the seemingly sheltered world of the kindergarten class in The Holy Family

Convent in Wrexham, which was run by the nuns of the Rosminian Order. During her first term, it was announced that the Bishop would be attending the Christmas Concert at the end of term. To her delight, Noreen was chosen to be a clog dancer. There was to be an interlude between the first and second parts of the nativity play and six girls were chosen to be Welsh girls, demonstrating the ancient Welsh art of clog dancing. One of the nuns had brought back six delightful miniature pairs of clogs from Amsterdam where she had been on a short holiday to visit her brother.

Kitty made a Welsh lady's outfit for Noreen – a labour of love – and Jack lifted her onto the dining table at home when it was finished, so that they could admire her in it. Noreen looked like a little doll, she was so young – but she really got into the part. All at once, she set about sweeping the table top with her broomstick made with real twigs, just like an adult. Kitty and Jack felt that that moment alone made worthwhile all the scrimping and saving they had done to pay the school's fees. When Noreen went through her sequence of simple steps, for their benefit, they couldn't have been happier. They clapped until their hands were raw after watching her routine no less than five times.

The evening of the concert arrived. The Bishop and the Bishop's secretary were seated right in the front row. To the nuns the Bishop was an iconic figure and they had impressed on all the children how honoured they were that he was attending and how they must put everything into their performance, really give of their best. The nuns were all in a twitter and their excitement rubbed off on the children.

As the first half of the nativity play drew to a close, Noreen and her friends were lined up in the wings by the nun who had trained them. The music started and they were off. All six girls clog-danced with great verve, but to Noreen's disappointment and surprise the Bishop and his secretary had turned around and were chatting to people in the row behind them, as if the interlude performance did not matter. Noreen had not been prepared with any strategy to cope with a situation like this. All she could do was, as the nuns had told her to do, put everything she could into every step, so she redoubled her efforts in the hope that the Bishop would face the front and the whole exercise would go as it was supposed to. She swung her right leg as high as it would go, kicking forward to make the desired click on the boards of the stage. Unfortunately, the swing of her leg was so powerful that her right clog was sent spinning in a perfect arc towards the audience. One of the Bishop's secretary's shins stopped the clog from doing any injury to anyone else in the audience, after it had bounced once in the place where the orchestra pit would have been, had there been one. His shin certainly felt the full force of the clog's momentum. The nun responsible for the clog dance quickly retrieved the errant clog and put it back on Noreen's foot. The Bishop and his secretary, as well as the rest of the distinguished audience, paid rapt attention to every minute of the remaining part of the performance. At the end, there was rapturous applause. The parents, invited guests, Mother Superior and the other nuns, all rose to their feet as one, and eventually even the Bishop and his secretary had to put aside their dignity and stand to applaud. The clog dance had brought the house down. There were a lot of laughs and indulgent smiles among the cheers, but happily the girls were too young to realise their impact had as much to do with their youthful appeal as with their dancing skill. So elated were they by the response, that they would have stayed on stage curtsying all evening, if their nun had not shooed them off the stage after their third curtain-call.

Her experience of participating in this live perform-ance left Noreen with a passion for theatre, drama, dancing, and singing. She was undoubtedly the most memorable performer at the Christmas Concert. Her energy, drive and enthusiasm could not fail to be noticed and she was far from being overshadowed by her five dancing companions.

NOREEN looks across the tops of the trees towards Penarth reflectively, as she is wont to do.

"Oh, I can remember how jolly angry I was with the Bishop. Funny, isn't it. Of course my father had a terrible temper too, especially when younger. I think that was why he never took over the farm in Ireland. Rowed with his father over something silly, which day to harvest the hay I think it was, and was too proud to stay working on the farm until it came his turn to take it on. A thing like that changes the whole course of your life, doesn't it? I might have been talking in a soft Irish brogue now, if he had stayed...

"You never really saw him like that, Cecil, did you? No, you didn't. He was quieter by the time you met him, I fancy. Oh yes, he was quite a hot head when he was young...

"I always remember him telling me about when he first started working in The Maypole after coming to live in this country. This other lad used to taunt him. Kept calling him 'Johnny from the country'. My father told me he caught him down in the cellar one day when he was getting some fresh cheese from the store and gave him a terrific hiding. The lad never taunted him again. I always felt it was so sad... that story. An opportunity lost to make a new friend. A lad his own age. But then I am not newly arrived in this country and do not speak with an Irish accent...

"He could be ruthless at home too. Not always the gentle-mannered man serving the ladies. I've told you about my pet rabbit, haven't I, Cecil? I have, don't shake your head..."

When Noreen talks, the way she projects her voice owes a great deal to her years of teaching experience, the need to entertain and maintain discipline at the same time, but it is equally the product of prolonged study of Speech and Drama, in her spare time.

"Your breathing has got to be right, you see... from deeeep down, using the diaphragm and inhaling through your nose... never your mouth." She believes with unswerving certainty that speaking properly is essential for good health and despairs of the future well-being of anybody whose speech is sloppy or who does not pro-ject each phrase in a fluent and confident fashion.

Cecil, despite his weakness now, projects each word and phrase with the maximum push he can muster. A lifetime of attending meetings has made him realise that how you say things is just as important as what you say, when it comes to making an impact on people. He did not get elected Grand Knight of the Knights of Saint Columba South Wales Branch on two occasions, by talking quietly at meetings. Not to mention his virtually continuous chairmanship of the Civil Service Catholic Guild for over fifty years, and his frequent role as Editor of the Archdiocesan Yearbook. He has made his points fully and frankly, in measured tones, always remembering that a bit of humour well-judged and appropriate to the occasion, the quizzically-raised eyebrow, self mockery about something trivial, or a cogent funny story – gets an audience on your side by breaking the tedium.

They say old habits die hard – some habits stay with us for a lifetime. Although there are rarely more than two or three other people in Cecil's room, both Noreen and Cecil continue to speak as if to a far bigger audience, even when only speaking to each other. It is what they are used to and it has the advantage that they are usually heard and usually hear each other. When Cecil addresses one of the care assistants, "I would like to use the toilet, if you please..." the dignity he maintains would not be out of place were he introducing eminent speakers at the end of a formal dinner.

When Cecil returns, Noreen's tale about her pet rabbit will not be denied. The rabbit's name, Coconut, so-called because of its wiry fur. Jack Byrne had never taken to Coconut. It had been nothing but trouble. A hutch had to be built at short notice, out of orange boxes from The Maypole, boxes which he had to carry home on his knee on the Crosville bus all the way to Rhosllanerchrugog. Jack loved his garden but he was not too skilled with tools. His carpentry was rough and ready, to say the least, and Coconut often found a way out of his enclosure to gorge himself on whichever of Jack's vegetables were in season at the time, however deeply Jack buried the wire netting which surrounded it.

Jack and Kitty had booked their first holiday, in a guest house in Aberystwyth. The evening before they were due to leave, they remembered they had not made any arrangements for someone to look after Coconut. It was too late to arrange anything. They were busy packing. They did not have a telephone. Kitty's relatives in Ellesmere did not have telephones either, so they could not use a public telephone. In any case, Jack was not concerned enough about Coconut to let making arrangements for him disrupt their first family holiday.

Jack no longer lived on a farm but he had been brought up treating animals as produce in the self-same way as any other crop. He was not sentimental about animals and did not like Coconut, who few would have described as an attractive rabbit with his door-mat fur and staring eyes. But Noreen thought he was attractive. In fact she doted on him. Her first pet. And she was convinced Coconut doted on her.

"You can guess what's coming, can't you, Cecil?"

Cecil shakes his head yet again.

"Do you think the ending might be different this time, darling?"

A shake of the head. It seems possible that Cecil is not actually listening – just making a random gesture at the end of each of the questions which come at him.

"No, it is not to be... Alas for Coconut – my poor Coconut – the ending is the same."

A tear is discernible in Noreen's eye, highlighted by the low, weak January sun, as she leans against the windowsill. Emotional still, over her lost pet. Or perhaps a composite, cumulative wave of sadness for all the farewells over the years of her lifetime thus far. Her mother, father, so many of her uncles, aunts and cousins and above all her fear that Cecil will not be here for ever, for long – a tough old bird, organically sound, could go on for months, years, outlive me, she thinks, but then again... And she thinks again of Coconut, her first, purest, simplest love. How her father, Jack, took him into their bathroom, the upstairs bathroom of which they were so proud. She imagines him putting the plug in the bath. Filling the bath half-full. Then, holding Coconut firmly by the ears, swinging the scrabbling creature up and over and into the water. She sees him holding Coconut under the surface of the water, easily at first, but being surprised by the strength Coconut showed in struggling. It must have taken more than a few minutes to do the deed, as Jack had sustained long scratches down the insides of his forearms by the time it was over. Noreen was already in bed asleep and knew nothing of it at the time. Her parents told her in the morning that Coconut had escaped from his enclosure again and there was no sign of him. The excitement of going away on holiday took Noreen's attention off her concern for Coconut initially, and her parents encouraged her to think he would manage to survive quite satisfactorily in the wild. A year or two later, their neighbour, Mrs Howarth, let it slip when talking to Noreen, by referring to "the day your father drowned Coconut..." When Noreen approached her mother about it, Kitty confirmed that that was what had happened, but Noreen never brought it up or discussed it with her father, right up to the day he died.

"I WENT to Ilminster Grammar School, you know." Cecil says to nobody in particular. "Do they still have Grammar Schools, do you happen to know? Comprehension Schools or some such thing these days..."

"*Comprehensive*, darling."

"Ah ye'm... I wonder if it's still going..."

Cecil closes his eyes. He is back at the old school. What was the Headmaster's name? Mr L. H. Mermagen. Or was it Mr H. L. Germamen? A fine man and a fine scholar, much respected by all his students and staff.

Old Mermagen had drummed into them the school motto at assembly, on their first day. In fact they were the first words he heard him speak, if Cecil remembers correctly... "'Learning Gayneth Honor', that's our school motto, gentlemen – never forget it!" On the second day, he had told them the long history of the School, since its foundation during the reign of Edward the Sixth, in 1549. And its purpose – so that the youth shall be brought up better knowing "...their duty as well to God as to the King's Majesty."

There had been three houses. Cecil was in Waldrond. The house into which all the Chard boys were put. The Ilminster boys and the boarders went into Wadham, and the boys from the general rural area were put in Hanning. It had been a formative experience of great value, Cecil recalls. Only 120 pupils in all. And exceptional examination results in the year he sat his examinations. His name and results, and those of his contemporaries, had been printed in the *Ilminster and Chard News*.

His old headmaster's name is on the School Certificate, in the locker somewhere, if only he can find it. Awarded by the University of Cambridge Local Examinations Syndicate. Or the University of Oxford Examinations Syndicate? Noreen took the one he didn't, whichever that was... Noreen always says she went to Oxford and he went to Cambridge, and they have a good laugh. Or the other way around. Darned if he can remember.

Sometimes when he has a heavy lunch – soup, a main course and his favourite sweet, jam roly-poly and custard – it makes him feel drowsy. Nods off sometimes.

Remembers the subjects he passed though. Same number as Noreen. Seven, he thinks. But higher marks, or lower in some and higher in others. Something like that. Noreen always remembers which. Religious Knowledge, English, English History, Geography, French, Elementary Mathematics, and Art. He also did Latin, Chemistry and Handicraft during his time there. He loves the smell of his certificate. He likes to think it's printed on parchment. It still smells of the school, chalk dust and polished corridors, all these years later. If only he can find it. Have a quick sniff. He opens his eyes. Noreen has gone. Maybe the certificate is in his locker somewhere, under the socks and the wintergreen? No. It must be at home. He will ask Noreen to bring it in, next time she comes. But he is sure it was The University of Cambridge Local Examinations Syndicate. And the Headmaster's name? L.H. Mermagen. Of course. That was it. He is almost sure. Good old L.H.

℘

"I WONDER HOW my friend Clare is now." Noreen sits on the edge of Cecil's bed, smoothing his counterpane with the flat of her hand. "You met her once, Cecil. Before we married. Remember?" Noreen gets up and busies herself with the vases of flowers along the windowsill in Cecil's room.

"Isn't she a nursing sister or something. On the box?"

"No, silly. That's Claire Rayner. I'm talking about Clare Kolb. My friend when I was at the convent school in Wrexham. Her father was the manager of the Wrexham brewery and they lived in that house on the brewery premises. They were German and with our lunch of cold meats we would all have a glass of lager in those elegant lager glasses with narrow bases which broaden out at the brim like a bell. My mother was shocked when I got home and told her the first time, but she was so impressed that they owned a car, she never forbade me from going there. Her father used to take us in the car to play tennis. It was a convertible. Some kind of Mercedes, I think. And we had huge fun wandering around the brewery. The workmen used to make ever such a fuss of us, and because Clare was allowed to do whatever she liked so was I. Of course, she was beautiful. She had this wonderful flaxen blonde hair and grey-blue eyes the colour of an air mail envelope and she had a very gentle nature. All the boys used to be after us, but I always knew it was because of Clare. They were attracted because of her looks, yet after a while some would get to like me because we would have a good laugh together. Do you remember her now, Cecil?"

"Long hair. Blonde, eh? Can't place her. Are you quite sure she works here?"

"I give up! It's my fault. Every day I keep meaning to bring your hearing aid in and every day I forget it. Of course she doesn't work here. She must be well into her eighties by now."

"Ye'm... I remember your father bringing us excellent ham from The Maypole grocery store during the war. But never serving us lager. That would not have been his style at all. Used to plunge a red hot poker into his glass of Guinness to mull it, I remember. Had never come across the practice before. Nor drinking a glass of port to accompany the Guinness. Too much really. But he had the build to take it. A solid citizen your father. There was no doubt about it. No doubt at all."

Noreen ruffles Cecil's hair, leaving on it traces of pollen from the stamens of the flowers she has just been rearranging, and a few tiny green fronds from their leaves.

"I often wonder how Clare is. Such a pity we lost touch..."

Noreen looks down again at Cecil from above. Not laughing this time. He is in bed today with a slight fever. She notices the pollen and fronds of green on his hair and a pang of tenderness shoots through her at his helplessness. She brushes them away.

"Still got a good mop of hair, C," she says brusquely. Noreen calls Cecil 'C' when she feels emotional and does not want to show it. It saves any wobble coming through in her voice when pronouncing Cecil in full, in the way she does normally, with a long drawn out emphasis on the first syllable of his name.

Noreen remembers reading somewhere that in a love relationship there is always one partner who loves and one who is loved. She wonders how it has been with them, after nearly sixty years together. Has Cecil been her love canvas on which she has constructed her love object, her man, her perfect partner? Has he been happy to be loved? To live his life in the re-assuring shade of her unending devotion. No, she thinks. We have been equals. To have and to hold. Joint bank accounts. Yet she can think of times when he has seemed not to see her even, as if totally wrapped up in a world of his own so complete that he seemed to barely regard her as a person at all.

"Do you, Cecil?"

"What? Still use Brylcreem?"

"No. Sorry. I was just thinking. Do you always think of me as a real person? You know – flesh and blood – as someone you really love?"

"What, dearest?" Cecil calls Noreen dearest, when he is being evasive. It annoys Noreen.

"Dearest, dearest! You know I hate being called that..."

"Sorry, wife! Is that better?" Noreen prefers this. At least it is meant humorously and is an objective description of Noreen's relationship to Cecil. "How do you mean – a real person...? Of course I do. Give me your hand." Cecil strokes Noreen's hand. He senses her need. Her uncertainty over what he feels emotionally, an uncertainty he sometimes feels himself. He blames his relationship with his father, Pop Connolly, for this but does not know why this should be so, or even if there is any validity in his assumption that this is the cause of the inner emptiness he sometimes feels, the panic and fear which threatens to overwhelm him. He strokes Noreen's hand. He nudges her wedding ring gently. "United... in marriage we are, aren't we?"

"Of course, husband!" Noreen sees the effort Cecil has made to placate her. The attention he has paid her. His concern, curving his body with considerable effort so that his head is raised. She withdraws her hand. He lies back. She places the palm of her left hand on his forehead. It feels a little too hot. She raises him to give him some water, then she leaves for she has some shopping to do for later in the day.

Cecil will not let a little fever bother him. When he learned at school that, in the year of his birth, Spanish flu was killing people off all around the globe – Asia, Europe, North America, China – one per cent of the world's population wiped out just like that, he came to regard his birth as a major triumph in the face of adversity, though obviously not through any effort on his part. Nonetheless, he feels fortune seems to be on his side in the business of living. So long as he keeps going, eating, breathing, sleeping, it goes on and on. There is no reason for it to end and no end in sight, so far as he can tell. Though he sometimes feels tired beyond anything he has experienced before, as if his blood is having to work extra hard to move around his body, it is not unpleasant and a nap usually sorts the tiredness out and gets the old red corpuscles flexing their muscles again.

Being born at the end of one World War and surviving a second World War unscathed undoubtedly left him relieved; he feels he has been the recipient of subtle intimations from somewhere that he should get on with the business of living. He is confident that a supernatural deity – simply God in Cecil's terms – is taking full responsibility for it all and it takes an enormous weight off his mind. So many other men die so young, he thinks. There was George Venables. The postman. His great friend for many years and staunch supporter in the Cardiff Civil Service Catholic Guild. A bachelor. Used to pop down to George's flat in Pontcanna to plan events on many an evening. There was that time they organised a pilgrimage to the shrine of Our Lady of Penrhys. Caught the bus all the way up to the Rhondda Fawr. They had good support for that trip. At least five or six attended. George, bald by thirty, dead by fifty four. Why?..

It must be time for tea now, surely, he thinks demandingly, looking for his alarm clock on his bedside locker. 4.30. It should be here by now. Noreen said she would be back at 5.30, as far as he can remember. There are things to look forward to, but why is tea late? He does not like it when tea is late. The catering staff sometimes spend too much time talking to other people in the hotel, on their way around. He has come across them on days when he has been in his wheelchair and become so impatient he has gone looking for them.

"Bon soir, mon cher. Ça va? Hein?" When Noreen returns after tea she is in ebullient mood. She has treated herself to some French perfume in Howell's department store in town. She leans down and kisses his cheek. "You like it?"

"Ugghh..." Cecil recoils involuntarily.

"You don't like it. A pity, *mon vieux*. But... *c'est la vie!*" She places her hand on his forehead. "You feel a lot cooler than you did earlier, anyway."

Cecil is in a large armchair next to his bed with a swivel table over his lap bearing his tea tray. A few stray crumbs of cake are still trapped in his moustache. Noreen brushes them into a paper serviette.

"So... how has your afternoon been?"

"Tea was late."

"Again! Oh, I'm so sorry... I know how that upsets you."

"Seed cake... too."

"Aghhh! Your poor dentures... Oh and I nearly forgot, I popped home on the way here and have remembered to bring your hearing aid in at last."

"Thank you," Cecil says courteously, placing the hearing aid on the farthest side of his locker.

Noreen seeks to distract Cecil from his disappointment over his tea by going through with him what she has bought in town. Bright red leather shoes with a low heel, a port-coloured dress with a suede belt, and an all-enveloping maroon shawl to go with it.

"How do you like them?"

Cecil flinches away chuckling, as if the colour is dazzling his eyes. Noreen dabs some more of the perfume behind her ears and starts talking about how it reminds her of the year she spent living in France. For some reason, when she was sixteen, the nuns in the convent school in Wrexham arranged for her to go to a convent in Mont de Marsan as an English assistant. There had been riots in Paris over the Stavinsky affair in the February, followed by a general strike throughout France. In Germany, Hindenberg died, aged 87, leaving the way clear for Hitler to become head of state. At the same time, unbeknownst to Noreen, Cecil was riding around the Somerset countryside on his first motorcycle, a 97cc Coventry Eagle, although he had yet to go abroad.

Noreen's parents, Jack and Kitty, thought the nuns were arranging for Noreen to go to the convent in Mont de Marsan because they regarded her as a talented scholar and hoped to help her fully develop her potential. They did not read the papers very closely, only the parts of the local paper which were of interest, like the Births, Marriages and Deaths. Jack's father, who had the farm in Baltinglass, was unable to write and marked Jack's birth certificate with a cross. Jack himself moved his lips when he read and spoke the words half-aloud. Noreen did not read the papers at all at that time and was blissfully unaware of events in Europe or the journey ahead of her, but was very pleased with the Parker fountain pen her parents gave her to encourage her to write home while she was away. She went all the way to the south of France, unaccompanied, on the train. Looking back on it she wonders if the Rosminian nuns in Wrexham thought she would make a good nun and were grooming her for the role. If that was the case, Noreen was having none of it. She tells Cecil she felt the most adventurous and healthiest in her whole life, when she lived there. She puts it down to the purity of the air, owing much to the closeness of the Pyrenees, the pine forests in Les Landes, and the warm climate. She says she explored the region as much as she could, into the town, to the bull-fights, down to the endless white beaches at the coast, cycling in the neighbouring countryside, anything to enjoy the experience to the full. She says there was a lot of praying inside the convent where she had to live, but that most of the nuns were very jolly and friendly when they were not praying.

ℬ

THE LUXURY APARTMENTS in Cardiff Bay are proving popular amongst Noreen's friends. She tries to keep her life as normal as possible, despite Cecil no longer being able to get out and about. People call her brave. She says she is a tough cookie, but not brave. She simply sees no point in giving up. She has been invited for a meal with one of her friends from the drama group, whose flat over-looks the Bay. Noreen enjoys donning her new red shoes and the new dress and shawl she has bought. After the meal they go out on the balcony for a short while, admire the boats bobbing at their moorings and the Norwegian Church like a brushstroke of white oil paint on the far side, but the January chill forces them back inside after a few minutes. She gets lost driving home. Most of the roads are new to her because of the extensive redevelopment, but once she has found Bute Street she is able to trace her way to the centre of the city and thence home.

Undaunted, she has maintained her links with the drama group for over forty years. She is a life member now. Has not played a part for a year or two. Not since she played Lady Bracknell in *The Importance of Being Earnest* – "A handbag... A handbag!" Always involved though, doing front of house for the summer Shakespeare productions in the Welsh folk museum at St Fagan's. Sometimes she cannot resist getting involved with preparing the costumes, using skills inherited from her mother.

While Noreen is at lunch, Cecil is in his room, mentally working through all the motorised conveyances he has ever owned. If one did not know what he was doing one might imagine Cecil was sucking slowly on a lozenge. He finds pursing his lips, making his cheeks concave and lifting his chin a little, conducive to good concentration. For a reason he does not understand, he can recollect the registration number of every vehicle spanning a period of 65 years, even though sometimes he cannot remember what he has eaten for breakfast, though Corn Flakes, toast and bacon and egg, are likely to have started his day. That is what he chooses every morning, despite the allure of such continental delicacies as croissants and muesli.

He is lost in a sensual reverie about the Enfield Silver Bullet which he owned between 1934 and 1935. Far more powerful than his first motorcycle, his Coventry Eagle. The Eagle's engine had a cubic capacity of only 97. Its registration plate was YD 579. The Bullet's engine had more thrust, a cubic capacity of two hundred and fifty. You really had to hang on and lean right over when you were cornering. Darn it, the number plate of the Bullet eludes him today. Must have flashed through his mind too quickly. Not to worry, it'll come back to him tomorrow.

What came next? A car. The first Austin Seven he owned. A lovely little runner. BPD 502. Never let him down. Used to take Pop and Mammy out for trips all over the place in that. Picnics by the sea. Lulworth Cove. Had a little Union Jack on the bonnet. Owned that from 1935 until 1937. It was the next Austin Seven he drove Noreen around in – 1937 until 1942 he owned that one. Did quite a lot of their courting in it. Lyme Regis – where there were different coloured seaweeds and you could walk out to the end of the Cobb and on a quiet day feel you were the only people in the universe. What was the registration of that one? No, it's gone. Not having a good day today, he thinks. Not for memory anyway. Didn't own another car then until 1958 or it could have been 1959. The old Ford

Popular. OTG 851. Got 60 miles per hour out of that going down that hill near Cowbridge. Stormy Down. That must have been around the time Noreen and he bought their first ever black and white television set. In 1958, or '59. Only one channel, BBC, at the time. Had wooden doors you could close when you were not viewing. More like a piece of furniture really.

෪

NOREEN AND CECIL attend Mass every day on the ground floor of what Cecil calls the hotel. There is a very old, retired priest living there like Cecil. Father Carberry. Noreen pushes Cecil down there in his wheelchair at ten o'clock. It is an old-fashioned wheel-chair. Heavy. She gets him into the lift. Along the interminable corridor on the ground floor. It is Cecil's main excursion of the day. The Mass sometimes takes a very long time, if Father Carberry has not slept well. He is very devout but spends minutes on end staring into space. Nobody knows whether he is praying silently or day-dreaming. Sometimes Mass is over very quickly, when Father Carberry leaves large parts of the service out by mistake. He went into the last gospel straight after the opening prayers on one occasion. It was simply a question of turning over too many pages of the missal and not noticing.

Noreen does not hoard things. She likes to get on with life. Let the past go. She never even tells anyone her age because she believes people will treat her according to their own preconceptions. She knows Cecil has a lot of things in his bedside locker that he regards as private and confidential. She knows he has quite a large black cashbox which he keeps locked and in which he keeps every single letter she ever wrote to him, amongst other things. She knows this because she saw inside it once years ago when he forgot to lock it.

No, Noreen does not hoard things, but at Mass every day she looks at two faded newspaper cuttings. They are from the *Chard and Ilminster News* of Saturday, July 2nd, 1938 and Saturday, July 9th, 1938. She keeps them in her missal and says prayers of sincere thanksgiving to God for the fact that she did not lose Cecil, when their love was just flowering in Chard. Cecil was working in his first job as a Post Office clerk in Chard Post Office when he succeeded in getting another job in Frome, 40 miles away, with the Ministry of Agriculture and Fisheries. The first article reads:

CHARD POST OFFICE PROMOTIONS

Congratulations have been extended to Mr. C. Connolly, who, in a recent Civil Service competitive examination, secured a high place amongst the successful candidates. There were considerably over 1,700 entrants.

Mr. Connolly has for several years held the responsible post of senior clerk at Chard under the supervision of his father, Mr. P. J. Connolly. Mr. C. J. Connolly is well known through his connections with the Chard Roman Catholic Church, and he is also hon. treasurer of the Chard branch of the League of Nations Union. His success will necessitate his leaving Chard to take up a higher Government appointment in the Ministry of Agriculture and Fisheries based in Frome, Somerset.

The second one reads:

PRESENTATION TO MR. C. J. CONNOLLY

Appointment to Ministry of Agriculture and Fisheries in Frome.

In the presence of a representative gathering of the local Post Office staff on Friday last, Mr. C. J. Connolly was presented with a handsome travelling bag on his leaving Chard to take up his new appointment at Frome.

Mr. E. A. Wainwright presided and referred in high

terms to Mr. Connolly's sterling abilities and to the happy relations which had existed, particularly during the time Mr. Connolly had been senior clerk. They were sorry to lose such an efficient officer – a loss shared by several organisations in Chard in which Mr. Connolly was actively interested. The Chairman said he felt certain the Ministry of Agriculture and Fisheries would quickly recognise Mr. Connolly's qualifications and all his old colleagues would look forward to hearing of his continued progress. (Applause.)

Area Postmaster (Mr. W. West), in presenting the bag on behalf of the staff and himself, endorsed the Chairman's remarks and expressed his personal regret at losing such an exceedingly good officer. He thanked Mr. Connolly for the great assistance he had rendered during the many recent local changes and alterations, congratulating him on his splendid achievement in the recent competition examination, and on behalf of the whole staff, wished him continued progress and happiness in his new work. (Applause.)

In thanking the staff for the present, which he said he much appreciated and valued, Mr. Connolly referred to the happy time he had spent at Chard. They had to thank Mr. West, Area Postmaster, for his departure, because it was he who urged him to take the examination which secured him his new appointment.

Mr. A. R. Trickey, on behalf of the outdoor staff, and Mr. T. L. W. Legg, on behalf of the younger members of the indoor staff, spoke very highly of Mr. Connolly's work and of his readiness to help his colleagues at all times.

Mr. Connolly's successor at Chard has not yet been appointed.

Noreen tried immediately to get a job in Frome. She made some enquiries through Reverend Mother at St Gildas'

Convent School in Chard, where she was teaching. She learned there was a Catholic High School in Frome. She sent off a hopeful letter of enquiry to the Reverend Mother at the Saint Louis High School. The reply was not from Reverend Mother herself. It was in a very neat hand:

Saint Louis High School,
FROME,
Somerset.
July 16th 1938.

Dear Miss Byrne,

I am very sorry that we have no vacancy for a teacher in the High School, and having had our present teachers for a number of years we are not likely to lose them for some time.

I do hope you will find a suitable post and assure you of my prayers for your success.

Yours sincerely in Jesus Christ,
Sister Gabriel,
pp. Reverend Mother.

At that point Noreen composed herself, reasoning that if Cecil loved her he would keep in touch. She might try to see if there were any suitable schools in Wells – that would at least be closer. And she told herself chance always played a part in these things. She would not even have met Cecil, had she not been living in Chard in the first place, and she would not have been living in Chard if her friend, Margaret, with whom she had attended the Endsleigh Teacher Training College in Hull, had not told her about the vacancy in Chard one glorious summer's day.

Margaret had obtained a post in Chard after qualifying in Hull. She and Noreen spent a week holidaying together in Torquay and it was only then that it emerged there was an additional vacancy for an elementary teacher able to teach French, Music, Drama and Physical Education. Noreen had jumped at the opportunity. Once she had qualified in Hull her parents had tried to insist that she should return to Rhosllanerchrugog to live with them. They had been more or less promised that the nuns in Wrexham would offer her a teaching post, if she returned to the area, and they were keen that Noreen should follow up a brief friendship she had established the previous Christmas with Eric McBride. Eric was the son of Jack Byrne's friend, Harold McBride, who owned a fish business in the centre of Wrexham, opposite The Maypole grocery stores. Eric would be inheriting his father's business in due course. Perhaps Jack did not want his daughter to make the same mistake he had in walking away from his inheritance.

Eric was undoubtedly presentable, a nice lad, and keen. But the situation was becoming increasingly embarrassing for Jack and Kitty. They were receiving regular visits from Eric, during which he would politely and repeatedly enquire after Noreen's health only to have to be told that Noreen was either not at home, or she was holidaying with friends, or she was just on her way out, or in her room with a slight migraine.

Noreen was an independent spirit by nature but her years spent in France and Hull had added considerable additional strength to this aspect of her personality, at a time when daughters were expected to do what their parents told them, especially parents who had found themselves required to fund their daughter's career to a considerable extent, from what was only a modest family budget. Noreen's independence was about to be compromised. She simply did not have the money to support herself and was thinking of capitulating to her parents' wishes, when Margaret told her about the vacancy in Chard. The job was not for what was called a 'Certificated

Post' and the nuns did not therefore pay a full salary.

However, not only did the job in Chard mean that Noreen was able to earn her own living, it meant that she knew someone in the school right from the start and their friendship helped both young women cope with being away from home in their first job. Although the nuns were undoubtedly extremely kind and willing to help with most things, Margaret and Noreen were able to avoid becoming dependant. Noreen did not want to live at home. Nor had she met anyone of the opposite sex to whom she was attracted. If Margaret had not been around, Noreen might have become increasingly attracted to the simple expedient of shutting herself away in the convent and giving herself to God.

‫ಬಿ‬

KNOWING THAT CECIL would soon be moving to Frome, Noreen came to look on the Grand Garden Fête of the 29th June 1938 as a symbol of the happiness they had shared up until then. There had been just two short months of intense joy and heightened awareness. For two months Cecil had been a short bicycle ride away. Now he would be several hours travel distant – with contact in future, if it took place at all, only possible at weekends and during holidays, and then there was spending time with parents to consider, hers and his – and hers lived at the other end of the world, at Rhosllanerchrugog. She came to regard those two months in 1938, May and June, as a cameo of perfection, a finished episode during which nothing could have gone better, like an insurance policy against future unhappiness – should it follow.

When the seeds of their romance were set, during their encounter in The Catholic Church Of The English Martyrs in Chard, there had been no doubt in Noreen's mind that this was the start of something big. Their initial cup of tea together in the Church Hall had been followed by trips to Cleeve Abbey – and a lovely drive over The Quantock Hills, a day trip to Glastonbury Tor where they picnicked on the top, and a long drive to Brent Knoll where they had another picnic and Cecil took photographs of the surrounding countryside.

"And did the countenance divine, Shine forth upon our clouded hills?" Cecil recited, whenever the sun came out.

Noreen began to notice how much he was drawn to things poking up from the landscape, not only hills but spires and steeples too. She liked this and saw it as an understandable reflection of his aspiration to move onward and upward, ever upward. Cecil was also fascinated by islands and he persuaded Noreen to sally forth with him on the short journey to Lundy Island, more to experience being on an island than to see the puffins, so far as Noreen could tell by Cecil's reaction. In fact Cecil had seemed quite fearful of the puffins, though Noreen found them cute. Noreen interpreted his intense interest in islands as indicative of Cecil's single-mindedness and strength of character.

How Cecil fitted everything in, Noreen did not know. He planned their days out like military campaigns, noting in great detail in advance all the roads, map references, churches and other places of interest which would combine to make for a fully-utilised day. The only thing which ever caused any difficulty was if the timings set down by Cecil could not be adhered to because of road works or, as occasionally happened, Noreen might want to stop the car on the spur of the moment, to go back to look at a suddenly-glimpsed view, or to pick flowers from a flourishing hedgerow. Then Cecil would pace around striving to keep his patience, trying to stop himself looking at his watch too often, making himself enjoy the view with Noreen or the picking of flowers, knowing that he should, but really wanting to move on so that they kept to his timetable. Noreen found all this part of Cecil's charm. She had never met anybody like him before. His principles, his energy, his infectious enthusiasm for all his hobbies and interests.

And, on top of all the other demands on his time, Cecil took on responsibility as one of the Joint Honorary Secretaries for the Grand Garden Fête. The aim was to reduce the debt outstanding on the church and, with Mother Superior's permission, would take place in the grounds of Saint Gildas' Convent. Most members of the parish, the parish priest, Father Mortlake, and the nuns and pupils at the convent were all to be involved. Sadly Father Mortlake was moving to Tewkesbury, but a new priest, Father O'Beirne, was coming soon.

Cecil's first task had been to write to The Hon. Muriel Fitzalan Howard, Clay Castle, Haselbury Plucknett, asking her if she would agree to open the fête. He had written to the honourable lady in March, before he had met Noreen – Noreen found it hard to imagine Cecil having any really meaningful existence before they met. The honourable lady had replied on distinguished-looking blue headed paper, "Yes, I have time on that date – Wednesday 29th June – down in my diary – I will keep it free. My phone number is Crewkerne 326, in case you want to discuss anything with me. Yours sincerely, Muriel Fitzalan Howard."

There had been meeting after meeting in the weeks leading up to the big day. Cecil had even managed to co-opt his father onto the committee and persuaded him to occasionally attend Mass on Sundays. Cecil was unstoppable. There was to be a Diadem Cake-Making Competition; A Baby Show; Stalls – Needlework, Fresh Produce, Ices and Drinks, Bran Tub, Book and Piety Stall, Teas, Skittles, Darts, Coconut Shy, Rolling Pennies, Hoopla, Swings, Bucket With Coin; Treasure Hunt; a Variety Concert; a Convent Entertainment organised by Noreen herself; and an Evening Dance.

The beauty of it was that all the planning gave Noreen and Cecil many opportunities to see each other, in the weeks before the fête. Only Noreen's friend, Margaret, knew of the friendship between Noreen and Cecil. Cecil had told nobody. It gave their meetings an added frisson, knowing the other was so much more aware of him or her than all the other people present, but not showing it. Noreen went to several meetings of the committee to discuss the performances the convent girls were going to give, and even to a meeting at Cecil's home. How she and Cecil laughed when he told her that his mother had said, "She seems like a nice young lady, Twas... Miss Byrne, was it?" After Noreen had left.

On the day of the fête, Noreen felt her heart sink as she watched Cecil rushing here there and everywhere – except in her direction. She was desperate for him to acknowledge her. She had to watch him standing beaming behind The Hon. Muriel Fitzalan Howard, as she declared the fête open, at 2.30pm. Then he was across at the Fresh Produce Stall, checking with Misses Philly and Pat Balcombe whether they had enough float in their petty cashbox. Then he was showing 'Little Leslie', the comedian from Yeovil, here for the variety show, where he could change in the convent gardener's shed.

The interval was an opportunity for the committee members to get together to check whether there were any hitches. All was going well, Noreen learned later, except that far more babies had been entered for the Baby Show than had been expected. At 2.45pm, the total number of entries stood at 75. By 3.00pm, the number was 120. At 3.15pm, entries had increased to 150. By 3.30pm, when entries had reached a staggering 200, the committee decided they could not accept any more, on the grounds that judging would never be complete if more and more babies kept arriving.

Noreen's girls were as good as gold. They sat patiently on the grass waiting until it was time to perform their entertainment. The weather had been kind and the grass was dry. They kept up a subdued hum of conversation as they watched the unaccustomed comings and goings throughout the normally tranquil convent grounds.

Noreen began to worry that Cecil would be too occupied with his responsibilities to watch her during the moment when she and her pupils would be the centre of attention. They were due to perform at 4.00pm. Just as she raised her baton to conduct the first performance, a dance piece entitled 'The Goslings' performed by the Senior Girls, she saw Cecil settle himself down on the grass at the side of the stage, right at the front. To her delight, he stayed put throughout 'The Flag Drill' by the Infants, 'Country Dancing' by the Senior and Junior Girls, 'Market Day' by the Preparatory Class, 'Danny Boy' the Seniors again, 'Ribbon Dance' the Juniors, and finally 'Land Of Hope And Glory' the Senior Girls Choir. As she conducted each piece and then directed the children on and off the stage, Noreen began to notice that Cecil's eyes seemed fixed on her, even when Lavender Harrison, an outstandingly beautiful singer from amongst the Seniors was performing her soprano solo during 'Land Of Hope And Glory'. Noreen was hugely flattered but greatly feared that her attention was wavering, and she so wanted to do her best for these girls who had worked so hard in reaching the standard they had – all 79 of them.

Noreen need not have feared. When Noreen and Cecil went on their next day out together to visit Wells Cathedral, they sat themselves down in a little tea shop. Cecil had with him the *Chard and Ilminster News* which they scanned avidly for anything about the fête. Sure enough it contained a very full report which stated that during the afternoon a most enjoyable entertainment was given by the pupils of the Convent School. "This had been admirably arranged by Miss N. Byrne..." Cecil's efforts had not been overlooked either. Special tribute was paid to Messrs. T. W. Sanders and C. J. Connolly, it being noted that they were to be specially complimented on their contributions to the success of the venture, which was described as one of the best supported affairs of the kind ever held in the town with the financial result, if anything, exceeding expectations. The final figure was not yet in but Cecil said the profit was likely to exceed the present total of 76 pounds, one shilling and sixpence.

Having established they were mentioned in the report, Noreen and Cecil were reduced to fits of the giggles as they read the headlines and the report of the Baby Show. The headline read – 'CHARD'S TINY TOTS – 200 on view at Convent Garden Fête'.

What was pronounced an outstandingly fine show of Chard's tiny tots – of whom 200, all under three years of age, were on view – was a feature of an enterprisingly arranged garden fête, bazaar and funfair at St. Gildas' Convent Grounds, Chard, on Wednesday. For two and three-quarter hours the judge, Dr. R. DeVeil King, of Taunton, was kept busy and not before six o'clock was it possible to announce the results. Dr. King, addressing the large gathering of parents, confessed that the judging had been very difficult. He had not expected quite so many entries and it showed what an interest was taken in infant welfare in the district. He announced that in Class A (up to 18 months), five babies had tied for first place, such was the standard of competition. In Class B (18 months to 3 years), prizes had been awarded for 1st, 2nd and 3rd places. "I was impressed," said Dr. King, "by the type and standard of baby, the standard of cleanliness and the general health of them, and I think there is a great deal of credit due to the mothers of the neighbourhood." (Applause.)

"Can you credit it, Cecil? So many babies in the same place, all at once?" Noreen and Cecil coughed and gurgled into their tea-cups helplessly, much to the disapproval of the good people of Wells who were drinking their tea all around them in a civilised fashion.

Between the sending of Cecil's invitation to The Hon. Muriel Fitzalan Howard on the 6th March, and her reply on the 19th March, Hitler annexed Austria to 'protect' ten million Germans living outside the Reich's frontiers. Between the garden fête and Cecil taking up his new post in Frome, Hitler had told his generals, on the 28th May, "It is my unshakeable will that Czechoslovakia shall be wiped off the map."

Cecil was too busy to take a lot of notice of what was going on abroad at the time. He was however proud of his active links with the League of Nations Union, whose honorary presidents were the Rt. Hon. Stanley Baldwin, M.P., the Rt. Hon. J. R. Clynes, and the Rt. Hon. D. Lloyd George, O.M., M.P.. Cecil had been working hard to keep the local study circle in Chard going over the winter, as encouraged by Lt. Col. G. N. Wyatt, D.S.O., the organiser in Bristol, but it had been uphill work. In the spring, he had given a talk to the local group but only three people turned up, all people whom he knew well. His talk was entitled 'War Clouds'. He expressed his grave concern over the continuing purchasing of machines of destruction because of the high probability that purchasing armaments could change, at very short notice and with calamitous results, into a war which would prove without doubt their effectiveness. He saw the need for an effective agreement to put an end to the continuing acquirement of arms. He felt it was a responsibility shared by each and every citizen to make their views known, in the interests of peace. He was hopeful that the dark cloud, which had hung menacingly over the horizon of Europe for so long, at last showed some signs of lifting. However, he remained very concerned that while Prime Ministers and Presidents were vying with one another in declaring their sincere desire to keep the peace, government after government, with few exceptions, were increasing enormously their expenditure on armaments. A sincere desire for peace he felt was what was most called for, not merely a display of hypocritical rhetoric. When he read to Noreen the talk he had given in full, she simply said she wished he could be the Prime Minister, but that she liked him well enough as he was.

February, 1999

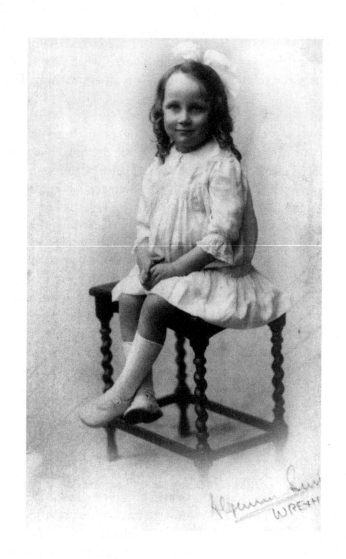

FEBRUARY IS THE MONTH of Cecil and Noreen's wedding anniversary. Like clockwork, when February comes, Cecil follows a little ritual. It is a private thing. His way of paying homage to their marriage. He gets out his locked black cashbox. Opens it with the key which he keeps in his wallet, and every day takes just one or two letters from the bundle he keeps inside the box. They are all letters Noreen sent him, before they were married. Every day, leading up to their anniversary, he reads the one or two letters he has taken from the box that day. The letters take him back to the roots of their relationship, when the heat of their mutual but restrained passion was so strong that he sometimes found it difficult to concentrate on ordinary things like servicing his car, without drifting off into a reverie about Noreen's beauty. Cecil has never told Noreen he reads her letters every year. He believes she may have guessed he does something of the sort, at least he thinks she knows he still has her letters because one day he forgot to lock the box. Noreen was in the room later and he found some of the letters had been disturbed. Cecil has never come across the letters he sent to Noreen during their courting years but he suspects she has them hidden away somewhere, and he would not be in the least surprised if Noreen did exactly the same as him each year.

This year, he recognises it will be a bit more difficult to read the letters in private. But he has noticed that in this hotel, although their timekeeping with tea is poor, there is often a long gap between Noreen bringing him back from Mass and taking herself off shopping and the arrival of lunch. In that fortuitous interval, he intends to find some privacy, if they do not take his cardigan for laundry without checking with him first, so that he can retrieve his wallet from its pocket and with it the key to the box.

The first letter always reminds him of Noreen's youthful charm. They had been to a whist drive organised by the Knights of Saint Columba. He had recently been elected the Deputy Grand Knight, an honorary position to which people were mostly elected for showing exceptional enthusiasm and commitment. Noreen had arrived in a tizzy because she had been delayed and had no money on her. She had been supervising a group of girls who had been playing netball against a neighbouring convent and got back late.

St. Gildas' Convent,
Chard.
15th May, 1938.

Dear Mr Connolly,

This one and sixpence has been on my mind since last Wednesday. I am sorry I was not able to pay my way at the whist drive – I had hoped to see you at choir practice the other evening (great that you've joined!) but I could not make it owing to some marking which I just had to do. I would have congratulated the Deputy Grand Knight if I had – you do sound imposing.

I sincerely hope the Knights of Saint Columba's funds have not collapsed through lack of my one and sixpence.

All best wishes for continuing success with the whist drives. I look forward to attending again and will bring some money next time!

I remain,

Yours sincerely,

Noreen Byrne.

Cecil replaces the letter, at the back of the bundle. They are all carefully arranged in chronological order, so the one dated 21st May, 1938, comes next. All is quiet. The cleaners have been around and done his room. He can just make out the sound of their Hoover, in a room along the corridor. There should be no further interruptions before lunch. Now, what was the second letter about? – Oh, yes, the cheeky one, where she makes fun of him being Deputy Grand Knight because he wouldn't come out of the Knights' meeting to speak to her because their deliberations are held in absolute secrecy.

St. Gildas' Convent,
Chard.
21st May, 1938.

Dear Peerless Excellency or rather Deputy Peerless, etc.,

I can assure you, I did not call you anything as nice as that last night – to think you could not manage to receive MY secret communication! And I thinking you were a tactician of the first order. All I wanted to do was give you my sub for Father Mortlake's what's-its-name – his farewell present. And while I'm on the subject, what he's going to do with a leather-bound copy of *An Imitation of Christ* at his age, I don't know? Really! Surely he's Holy enough? In my opinion, a train ticket for the Blackpool Illuminations in the autumn would have cheered him up far more, don't you think?

Anyway, I do want to contribute to the collection you are making, but you would have been cutting it very fine had you not got something off me soon as I am likely to be broke by Saturday, so I am enclosing it herewith.

Many thanks for the book and the accompanying note. You will be relieved to learn you have redeemed yourself in part, and you are still my closest confidant, whereas I might have chosen Eric!

Au revoir,
Noreen Byrne.

What was the book? Of course, *Le Voyageur Sans Baggage*, by Jean Anouilh. He hadn't read it then and he still hasn't read it. Came across it in George's bookshop in Bristol. He knew Noreen liked French books. It seemed the obvious choice. He remembers asking her, "Is she well regarded as a writer in France, Anouilh?" Silly mistake. He wasn't that bad at French. Carelessness really. "He's a chap," Noreen said, in a totally matter-of-fact manner which Cecil felt was marvellous. He felt no embarrassment, when he could have felt absolutely wretched. He was always blushing at the time, although in some ways he gave the impression of being confident. That made it more difficult. His cheeks used to burn, especially when in the presence of the opposite sex or when he felt he had made a fool of himself. Noreen was so accomplished in so many ways, she could have been a real prig if she had not been so nice. She could talk fluent French, play the piano like an angel, sing, dance; she was a brilliant actress and she spoke with such authority, always so poised. She inspired him, made him feel so much more confident about those things he could do well. No wonder her pupils in the convent school adored her.

He would never have had the confidence to write an article on a topic of social importance, before he met Noreen. A topic you had to think about. He had always been based at home, until he moved to his appointment in Frome. But he realised how much harder it was for Noreen. Living in Chard because she wanted to follow a career away from her home area. A qualified teacher, wanting to teach in a Catholic School, but unable to live independently on her salary from the nuns. They reckoned the free accommodation she was provided with was sufficient recompense for the inadequate salary she received. At least, as a man, Cecil received a reasonably fair remuneration for the work he did, 25 shillings a week. Noreen had to get by on thirteen shillings and sixpence.

He remembers sweating blood composing the article. It was called 'Some Remarkable Facts', and it began...

The subject of Equal Pay For Equal Work has recently been much in the limelight. When this question is being considered, the phrase is usually interpreted to mean that if a particular task is performed by female labour the remuneration payable should equal that to which a man would have been entitled had he performed the same work. But does anyone ever stop to consider the effect of unequal pay on women's day to day lives? For instance having to buy inferior food and less of it. Their children suffer as a result. Also, the development of women's careers can be seriously blighted and even decisions about their very domicile can be dictated by iniquitously unfair pay arrangements...

Cecil managed five hundred words of what he considered incontrovertible logic and forwarded them to *The Times*. The Editor thanked him for his submission but pointed out most subjects of this nature were addressed either by the paper's staff writers or by academic experts of one sort or another. He felt many of the points Cecil made were very interesting but that, regrettably, the climate was just not quite right for an article of this sort. He thanked him generously however for taking the trouble to submit it, and said he hoped to see something from his pen again in the near future, which Cecil thought was very nice of him.

Lunch is later than usual arriving. It has usually arrived by 12.30pm. Still, it gives Cecil a chance to read another letter.

Dear Cecil,

How are you? Well, I hope. Thanks for your letter. It was nice of you to say you enjoyed yourself so much. I enjoyed myself too, very much. By the way I am probably creating a record. Never within the memory of living man have I answered a letter by return. If my many correspondent friends could know of it, they would probably come and tear you or me limb from limb, or rather "us" as you so gracefully put it in your letter (when referring to how you think about things now). It is of course quite crazy – but then I never did have much sense.

It is true, I would not mind your name being different. Of course, I realise it is too late now and I am accustomed to it, you poor old Cecily thing, but it really is a pity you weren't christened Padraig Joseph Connolly or something solid like that. What a shame your extraordinary precocity was not manifest at the baptismal ceremony and you could have piped in childish tones (so soon to lower to a resounding bass baritone), "Not Cecil... Not Cecil... Padraig Joseph, please..." Talking of which, have you read G.K. Chesterton's essay on giving everyone a number when they are born which they use until an age is reached when they can make their own choice over which name they want to use? It would be great fun – imagine me teaching... "472933, if you don't stop talking to 452 immediately, I'll make you sit by 57698!"

Now to the serious business!... About how things went after I got back to the convent, and whether there was any reaction from Mother Superior. They were all at supper when I got in and provided me with mine almost immediately. There was an atmosphere of great expectancy in the air, it seemed to me. I told them I had been to Yeovil Convent so, of course, they were interested in all the news I had to purvey. I also casually mentioned who I had been with – which occasioned no very great stir. I thought it just as well to mention it since Father Mortlake knew how I got to Yeovil and I did not want it to get back here through the tortuous method of Father Mortlake – Yeovil Convent – Chard Convent, as it inevitably would.

I am looking forward to my forthcoming long weekend trip home – heavenly thought – for a rest as much as anything else. I had better return on the Sunday afternoon, though, as probably we will have completely forgotten each other's existence after such a gargantuan separation.

But until Tuesday, I am, Yours,
Noreen.

It takes Cecil back. How keenly the nuns used to monitor Noreen. Hardly let her out of their sight. You would have thought she was one of the pupils, not a member of staff. Still, he thinks, they felt they were acting in her interests and to a large extent saw themselves as *in loco parentis*, with Noreen's parents living so far away. And it was fun, at times. He remembers struggling to help Noreen back into her room through a window she had left open in case it was needed. Luckily her room was on the ground floor. Cecil's heart pumps a little faster at the thought of the exertion involved and the ever-present chance that they would be discovered. He has read three letters on this first day. More than his usual one or two per day. Although he feels pretty robust all things considered, he tells himself he must not overdo it. Not at his age. He must rest. And lunch will be arriving, if not soon, sometime.

ॐ

IT BECOMES something Cecil looks forward to each day, that time when Mass is over and Noreen has left after her first visit of the day. The time when he looks through the letters. They have never before meant quite so much to him as they do this year, having so few of the things that are important to him to hand, apart from his private papers and some other small items he has in his bedside locker. He takes a letter dated Monday, July 18th, 1938. How well he remembers that time. New in his digs. 54, Somerset Road, Frome. New in his job. No parents around. No familiar people. No Noreen. How Noreen's letters used to affect him. Just the sight of them. Her handwriting. Spying the letter arriving on the doormat, he would have to stop himself from rushing forward, grabbing just his letter and retiring to his room to devour it immediately. Sometimes the other boarders picked the mail up. It would be left in a pile on the breakfast table for people to nonchalantly flick through as they talked over their toast and marmalade. The letter on the 18th July was special because it was the first letter Cecil received from Noreen after he moved to Frome.

St. Gildas' Convent,
Chard.
18th July, 1938.

My Dear Cecil,
I hope you do not have to take this out and read it at the breakfast table or your fellow boarders will think you have very inelegant correspondents. But since I had no note-

paper it was a toss up whether I should write on these sheets torn from an exercise book, or not at all – I choose what I hope you will consider the lesser of the two evils.

Many thanks for your letter. I was glad to observe the cheerful tone of the whole, I think you are going to like Frome – but I'm sure I shan't, horrible place taking you away from me!

Actually, I meant to write to you on Friday but Father O'Beirne, (the new young priest here in Chard, who has replaced Father Mortlake – you'd soon get out of touch if I didn't write wouldn't you?), anyway, Father O'Beirne came back up here again to the convent and of course we played tennis until 9.50p.m. with Margaret, the Balcombes, and Paul Smith. I don't think Mother Superior was overly impressed with what she seemed to feel was a rather feckless streak in Father O'Beirne. Still, it's early days isn't it? I think one should take into account he is new here and still doing his best to settle in. The tennis was great fun, it was quite like old times. Paul is frightfully vicious though. He wonked a ball on to Philly Balcombe's arm and nearly paralysed it. She has been going around with it in a bandage ever since.

By the way, did you know, Paul is quite amusing? I laughed myself sick at his adroit and amusing 'asides' – I really don't think we were serious enough for Father. He wanted to play very seriously, he is extremely competitive and worked up quite a sweat.

Did you, I wonder, pass through Chard at about 7.15p.m. yesterday evening? I guessed you might, on your way back to jolly old Frome. You would not have seen me though I'm afraid as I was a few miles away up at Buckland St. Mary and did not get back to the convent until late, 8.55p.m.(!), even then all the sisters were in bed and Sister Mary had had to wait up for me; but I did not mind so much, neither did she cast a reproving glance, because after all I was in 'respectable company', with the Balcombe family.

All this weekend, I have had a beastly sore throat and foul

cold, I almost lost my voice on Saturday. I don't know how I got it, but I feel inclined to blame you.

Are you visiting your parents again next weekend? Unfortunately I shall be very pressed for time because we shall be starting school exams, just ordinary terminals, next week so I shall be preparing exam questions in my spare time over the weekend. But, of course, I MIGHT be able to manage it on Saturday afternoon and evening!

Well, Margaret has just come into my room and is sitting on my bed demanding attention, so I must leave you. Thank you ever so much for the wild flowers. They are sweet. Gosh! You had some courage picking the ones on the river bank, didn't you?

Goodbye, my sweet, and good luck.

Love

Noreen.

There is a second letter in the same envelope. Cecil remembers he stored them like that because they arrived so close together, the second only two days after the first.

St. Gildas' Convent,
Chard.
July 20th, 1938.

My Dear Cecil,

I really AM busy this week and I really should not be writing this, since it is school time, BUT –

You will see by enclosed that I have had an answer from Saint Louis High School, Frome, from a Sister Gabriel. A nice little note but the answer is 'Non' all the same. I was not really disappointed (in one way) because I always felt, somehow, that it was pretty hopeless. Never mind, perhaps nice Father Metcalfe whom you were telling me about in your last letter will be able to do something, probably not by next term, but perhaps after Christmas? I noticed in 'The

Universe' this week a vacancy for an uncertificated mistress at Wells Catholic School, so there must be a Catholic Elementary School there. I think I shall write to Father McEnery about it. He seems to know everything there is to know about Catholic Schools. Usually Elementary uncertificated jobs are fairly decent, if not wonderful, and there is a chance of a certificated post turning up, once you are established. What do you think of this proposal?

Father O'Beirne must be going away today as he heard Confessions last night. Father Corr, his new assistant priest, has not yet full powers for hearing Confessions. I wonder what the rest of the Parish will do if it suddenly wants to go to Confession while he is away?

Do you know that to me Saturday seems years off, because I have so much to do. I have just been adding millions of marks up, tearing my hair trying to settle sets for the tournament, and endeavouring to think up some new ideas for the Treasure Hunt. In addition I have to pack – real packing for these long holidays and here I am spending precious time writing to you – but then you are more precious than my time! But I must go, so au revoir until Saturday outside the Cloaks.

All My Love
Noreen.

Cecil recalls that the Cloaks were at the local Palais de Dance. Always a good crowd there on a Saturday. Noreen had been the one who loved dancing, not him. Cecil thinks back and recognises that over the years he has changed in some ways, here and there. He has slowed down a bit. Well it is undoubtedly true he has slowed down a bit, he laughs sadly to himself. He has probably hardened his views in some areas, relaxed in others. But in one area of his life he has remained unalterably constant. He has always hated dancing, still hates dancing and always will.

He had never been to a dance until Noreen insisted they went, one dire weekend. At first he thought he was going to enjoy it. After all, he was with Noreen and that is where he wanted to be. The music was tolerably easy on the ear. The Big Band sound was new and becoming all the rage. A bit fast and jazzy but harmonic. People found it exciting. Cecil remembers nodding his head up and down, trying to appreciate the beat, while they had a lemonade at one of the tables around the dance floor. He could not really say it excited him, but it was interesting, different from most of the music he knew. Noreen kept leaping to her feet and doing one or two steps before sitting down again.

Eventually, Cecil remembers with a sinking heart, Noreen could wait no longer. Even now, sitting alone so many years later, Cecil cringes at the thought. Up Noreen jumped, tugging Cecil onto the floor, leaving their lemonades to go flat. She had done lots of practice, waltzes with the nuns on weekday evenings, and jazz-dancing to Margaret's gramophone in her room. Cecil had never even thought about how people danced. Looking back he realises he had always made a vague assumption that once you got on the dance-floor it somehow happened – arms, legs and body in harmonious and fluent accord with the music. It did not happen for Cecil. His legs became suddenly aware that they had ankles and knees, ankles and knees which were uncertain whether to bend, jump, jerk or freeze. Mostly they froze. Cecil tried to grasp Noreen's hand to turn their encounter into a kind of waltz in which there could be at least a scintilla of co-ordinated movement between them, but Noreen was driven, impelled by a manic energy – kicking, thrusting, leaping, even shouting in places, "Go, baby, go."

It was a total disaster. Cecil found the unpredictable journeyings of the other dancers disconcerting. Some gyrated in one place. Others seemed to feel their enjoyment depended on how much of the dance floor they could cover, and kept bumping into people, especially people like Cecil who were virtually motionless. Eventually, Cecil became totally transfixed, a helpless smile on his face, waiting miserably for the song to end. Luckily Noreen had been so caught up in expressing herself through the music she hardly noticed Cecil's discomfiture. "Another?" she suggested, breathlessly. Cecil declined, hastening for the sanctuary which the tables bordering the dance floor provided. He did not mind Noreen and Margaret enjoying themselves – they were up and away again immediately – but he knew that even if he practised until the seas ran dry he would never, never ever, enjoy dancing.

Resourceful to the end, and determined not to let Noreen down, after his first disastrous experience, Cecil got Noreen to map out the footwork he needed to be able to dance. By the time she was finished Cecil had a plan he could follow, not unlike the diagrams by means of which he turned out such beautiful fretwork. At home he practiced hard in his room. It was difficult without music. He had no gramophone. And Mammy and Pop Connolly kept tapping on his door and asking if everything was alright. But at least he was able to develop a sequence of steps which he was able to repeat ad infinitum and adapt to virtually any tune which the bands played. He added his own touch of swinging both hands to left and right, whilst turning his head in the other direction, which he hoped added a bit of originality to his performance. Nobody told him it didn't, so he persisted with it and, in conjunction with Noreen's step plan, it seemed to serve him quite well.

When Noreen comes in to visit him, Cecil does not bring up these old, treasured memories, the joy, the pain, the jealousies, the embarrassments, the laughter, the tears;

he just smiles in greeting. Noreen seems the same to him as ever. Were they to bring the Glenn Miller band into this hotel at this very moment, Cecil thinks, Noreen could still give a good account of herself. Would dance into the early hours, if they would let her.

Instead, they talk quietly about who Noreen has seen, where she has been, if the house is alright, how their son, Sean, is getting along, whether tea was on time or not. Cecil does not want to be thought of as living in the past. His philosophy has always been to press on, look ahead, never waste a minute.

"It's our fifty-ninth wedding anniversary this year, C," Noreen says brusquely one day, hiding any trace of emotion.

"Ye'm... Very good, wife. Yes, you've been a very good wife. All my life. Haha! I'm a poet, aren't I, and only you know it?"

"Mmmm... We'll have to do something to celebrate, won't we? It'll be harder this year, but we'll think of something, won't we?"

"Ye'm... Well, well. 59 this year, is it?"

MARRIED 59 YEARS. It seems like yesterday to Cecil. Another new day arrives. He pulls his cashbox towards him to read the next letter. It was the end of the summer holidays, he remembers. One of the good things about Noreen's job. Long summer holidays. And Noreen had been able to stay not too far distant, with friends in Somerset for much of the time, after having first spent a fortnight in Rhosllanerchrugog with her parents.

Cecil does not admit to any varying of emotion in relation to Noreen on his part, once he had fallen in love. One day he was a single man. A man with quite frequent yearnings to find a mate, but with no practical experience of being in love with another person. Then, on one particular day in May, he found himself to be in love, and that was a state which to his mind had never changed, varied, flickered or altered in any way whatsoever. There had been no reason for it to do so. Noreen was all he desired and from that particular point in time, she had been his constant soul-mate. He dates falling in love to the day in May when Noreen banged him on the head with Our Lady's banner. It was not love at first sight. He had needed some time to absorb the experience of their first encounter and to think about how well they had got on over a cup of tea in the church hall afterwards. It was not until the evening of that day, following a wholesome and restorative supper provided by Mammy Connolly, that he decided he was definitely, indubitably, fully and finally in love with Noreen, always would be, and would be unable to live on this earth without her from that time forward. Knowing what Noreen's feelings were towards him became a constant concern to him. He never felt complacent. In fact he spent long hours certain that he was deluding himself that someone as desirable as Noreen could harbour any affection for someone as unworthy as him, let alone be madly in love with him. Even now, all these years later, he finds the content of Noreen's letters far more than entertaining; you could call them my lifeblood, he thinks, yes, my lifeblood. He rubs the sheets of the letter between his dry, slightly-rough fingertips and notices how the texture of the paper feels just as it did in 1938, the words still fresh on the page:

St. Gildas' Convent,
Chard.
Tuesday, September 13th, 1938.

My Very Dearest,

It is so hard trying to WRITE to you after HAVING you. I think I agree with you that letters are very inadequate, but they must suffice for a little while yet.

The first day of term is over, and it really was not too bad at all, in fact I rather enjoyed it. It is quite a change to be doing something after doing nothing for so long. There is undoubtedly a lot to be said for 'doing nothing'; for behold, you return with a renewed zest for work, ready to enjoy getting down to the grind. I'll bet anything that today you tripped to the office with a heart full of eager expectancy, greeted your fellow workers with delighted effusion and begged to be given as much work as possible. I can imagine all your bubbling energy being directed into useful channels after your recent whole week of beneficial laziness. Nevertheless I hope that you were not so occupied that you did not miss me sometimes, a little bit.

As far as I can gather, the Chard news is practically nil. Father O'Beirne tells me there has been no Choir during the holidays because the Sisters were away on some sort of religious retreat.

One thing which APPALLED ME on my return was Father O'Beirne's hedge and lawn – you should just see it, it is like a tropical forest. He has not cut it once since he was here, as far as I can remember. The whole garden is like a great uninhabited wilderness! However he has achieved something. You remember Mrs Galpin, little Bernard's mother? Well, she was received into the Church at the beginning of the month and is still continuing with her instructions, so in all probability the husband will come back now. You know I can't help admiring Father O'Beirne for that, he really does go out after the 'black sheep' of his flock, even if he makes the white sheep bristle a bit from time to time.

My head simply swims when I think of all the things that demand my immediate attention and since I have not got you here to wheedle me into staying longer, I must go.

I do hope you got back safely and comfortably, write and tell me all about it.

Before I go I must say something 'nice' – but it is not to please you, it is just that I want to say it. You know during this last week my affection – no, my love for you has strengthened and deepened a hundredfold – Please God it will always be so.

And now, dear heart, goodbye and God bless you.

All my love

Noreen

ଛ

THERE IS SILENCE between Noreen and Cecil today. Noreen is tired. She had decided to go shopping before coming in to see Cecil and had bought him a white cardigan in a nice cable pattern because she had noticed yesterday that his maroon one was sagging at the elbows.

Cecil had not been happy putting the new cardigan on before going down to morning Mass. He repeatedly pointed out that his old maroon cardigan had a lot of life left in it and wondered aloud what he would do with the old one, if he were to start wearing the new one? He had not actually said he did not like the new cardigan but was worried that they could not afford it, and, fingering the white cable design disdainfully, kept murmuring as if to himself that his cricketing days were gone, long gone, in the full knowledge that Noreen knew he had never played a game of cricket in his life.

Noreen had ended up having to rush to get down to Mass in time because of all the palaver involved in getting Cecil to put the new cardigan on. His wheelchair had felt particularly heavy. Noreen had had to push it faster than usual and this had given her a pain in her lower back and left her feeling flustered. When, eventually, they had arrived in the room where Mass was to be celebrated, they discovered they need not have rushed. Father Carberry was having a bad day and had not yet come down. There was an air of stagnation and apathy pervading the room. Several nuns were on their knees praying with heads bowed. Most of the other hotel residents, Cecil noticed, were either very tired or actually asleep. Not very respectful, thought Cecil. Not when Mass was about to begin. As it turned out, Father Carberry was found to be having such a bad day that he was not able to come down at all and they all had to return to their rooms without having heard Mass.

Noreen does not like missing Mass. It gives her a sense of completeness to have been part of the familiar, reassuring ritual. The priest's arms outstretched as he turns to the congregation – "The Lord be with you..." The congregation's grateful response, "And also with you..." As much part of her life as combing her hair and brushing her teeth. As Jesus said, "Do this in memory of me..." Century after century. In Latin. Dark and mysterious for aeons. Then in English. Priest and congregation actually communicating with each other, mutual support and hope in a few well chosen words, "Let us lift up our hearts..." "We have raised them up to the Lord..."

Missing Mass, even on a weekday, leaves her feeling somehow incomplete, as if the day has not been blessed and she has not made herself worthy of God's care and attention on that day.

Cecil does not like to miss Mass either but, because he experiences time and events in a more haphazard fashion than Noreen, he is never quite sure whether he has been to Mass or whether they are about to go down at any minute. For that reason, Cecil is less concerned about things today than Noreen is.

She is quiet, he notices. Not as chatty as usual with stories about who she has seen, what she did yesterday evening, where she has been this morning. Oh yes, he remembers fleetingly, she has been into town this morning. Shopping. Where she bought him his new white cardigan. He watches and waits for her to turn away from the window at which she stands, leaning back slightly, her hands pressed against her lower back. He looks at her fondly, as one might at a favourite and familiar painting, at her auburn hair glowing in the harsh square-panelled light above her. Hair which retains as majestic a sweep and fullness of healthy growth as it ever did. Made more alluring if anything by the various tints and changing shades of colour which appear over the weeks following a hair-do, until the time comes to go again, when isolated silver-shining hairs have begun to mingle with her, by this time, reddish-brown, almost ginger, hair.

A poem which Noreen wrote out for him, when they were young, flows soothingly through his mind. Poetry has very little use, he thinks. But the sound the words make, he finds, is hypnotic, and some poems, just a few, if you say them repeatedly, over many years, begin to affect you in a way that you never really thought possible before. He does not say the words aloud but hums the syllables to himself. Written by a top man, too. A poet laureate – "Mmm Mmm Mmm MmmMmm Mmm MmmMmm Mmm..."

So sweet love seemed that April morn,
When first we kissed beside the thorn,
So strangely sweet, it was not strange
We thought that love could never change.

But I can tell – let truth be told –
That love will change in growing old;
Though day by day is naught to see,
So delicate his motions be.

And in the end 'twill come to pass
Quite to forget what once he was,
Nor even in fancy to recall
The pleasure that was all in all.

His little spring, that sweet we found,
So deep in summer floods is drowned,

I wonder, bathed in joy complete,
How love so young could be so sweet.

"...Mmm Mmm Mmm Mmm Mmm Mmm Mmm
Mmmmm..."

Cecil disagrees in his heart of hearts with the sentiment
of the poem. His love has remained constant, unchanging.
Anything different would not have made sense. And
anyway, how can one describe how much love one is
feeling, he asks himself for the thousandth time? It is not
possible.

Noreen turns away from the window. Looks straight
across at Cecil.

"You saying your poem, again?"

"No!... Er, well, ye'm. I was actually."

Noreen moves to the armchair beside Cecil's wheelchair. She takes his left hand with her right hand and
interlaces her fingers in his. What have I done to deserve
him, she smiles to herself? A man who says the same
poem over and over, even though he disagrees with what
it says.

There have been moments, Noreen reminisces silently,
brief and enigmatic admittedly but moments nonetheless,
when Cecil has seemed to rise to levels of imaginative
vision far beyond her; and she is supposedly the artistic
one, with her interests in drama, reading, writing and
music.

She remembers a distant Saturday afternoon. A white,
molten sun in a cloudless sky. They had planned to drive
over to Sherbourne together, to visit the Abbey there.
Neither had been before and Cecil said the Austin Seven
could do with a long run.

It was one of those still, breathless days, when the air is
so rich and pure that breathing it is like feeding on the
stuff of life, and everything is so obviously perfect you feel

weak at the knees with helpless frustration at your inability to preserve the day, other than in memory, so strongly do you yearn that it will last forever.

On the way there, they had stopped for a cream tea at Mrs Baverstock's tea rooms in Yeovil. By the time they had eaten that, chatting sixteen-to-the-dozen about the previous week's events; and had taken a leisurely stroll around Yeovil and then found that the car's radiator needed topping up, a task which necessitated buying and consuming a bottle of ginger beer and finding a shop willing to fill it up with water; the sun, though still high, was lower in the sky, preparing to steep the landscape in an ethereal golden glow before, as night fell, sinking down in a strong, monochrome sunset.

But as they drove into Sherbourne the sun was still very hot and the sunlight dazzling. The honey-coloured limestone of Sherbourne Abbey seemed alive to Noreen, not grey and forbidding as so many historic buildings seemed to her to be. Like something organic, expanding, growing out of the earth, a giant ochre fungus – looking good enough to eat.

Inside the Abbey, it was considerably cooler. Noreen recalls fondly how, without a word, Cecil slipped his jacket back on. Always prepared, and anxious to do the right thing. She assumed he did it out of respect for the fact that they were in a place held sacred by so many human generations and dedicated to the glory of God. She recalls how, for her, entering the coolness, peace and tranquillity of the Abbey, after the intense heat outside, evoked a surprising spiritual response within her, which coincided with, but far exceeded her sense of relief at feeling physically cooler. A realisation came to her that there is something more, beyond the immediate, the striking, the obvious. Beyond how we habitually see things and the demands and desires of our frail human frames. Something deeper under the surface. A presence, an echo, a held breath, an exhaled breath, of a power greater than us. She could only describe it to herself as a spiritual experience. An inadequate description, but it had been an experience ultimately beyond verbal definition.

She cannot remember all she and Cecil saw and did inside the Abbey, but her abiding memory is of Cecil standing beneath the breathtaking fan vaulting of the nave. She remembers he stood for a long time, his spectacles glittering on this day of exceptional light.

"I think they are like archangels' wings," he said.

"I do, too," Noreen had replied, feeling there was nothing further she could add. She could see what he could see, she thought. The coloured-glass sweep of the vast Perpendicular style windows, leading up to the curving fan vaulting which hovered tantalisingly above them, and through and beyond to the limitless sky high above, edged somewhere with the merest hint of feathered clouds, stretching into a far distance which cannot be fathomed, but only glimpsed.

The following weekend, Noreen remembers vividly, as she strokes the back of Cecil's hand with her free left hand, they sought to repeat the experience.

They decided they would travel together to Salisbury, to see the Cathedral there. Noreen remembers it vividly because, although the weather was nearly as nice as on the previous weekend, the experience for her was singularly different.

Cecil had taken out a book from the library during the week and done some background reading on Salisbury Cathedral. As soon as they arrived, Cecil was able to tell Noreen how construction of the Cathedral had commenced in 1220 and been completed by about 1360, a relatively short period of time which explained the fact that Salisbury was completed exclusively in the austerely elegant Early English phase of Gothic architecture and was not an amalgam of differing architectural styles across many centuries as so many Cathedrals are. As the result of Cecil's prodigious knowledge of the Cathedral's history, Noreen was deprived of one of her main pleasures when exploring old churches and cathedrals, that of reading all the plaques, tombstones and explanatory notices which usually adorn the walls of such ancient places of worship.

All was not lost, Noreen decided, when they went outside and stood brushing elbows, looking up in wonderment at the famous spire. They paused like this for several minutes without speaking, Noreen rather hoping that Cecil would make a comment as inspired as the one which he had made the previous weekend. Some coal-tits busied themselves nearby, flitting to and fro on a nearby grave stone. A magpie, thinking there was something interesting going on, chased them away and hopped around pecking at grass tufts at the base of the tombstone. Noreen held her breath for more than a minute at a time, not wishing to break the spell.

"One hundred and eighty feet tall – the spire," Cecil announced, finally.

"Is that all?" Noreen could not resist being catty, such was her disappointment.

Cecil had missed the irony in her tone.

"No, actually, a hundred and eighty feet is quite tall. And, incidentally, Noreen, this spire has a declination of twenty nine and a half inches in its alignment, but luckily it has not got any worse since Sir Christopher Wren measured it two hundred and fifty years ago."

"You do know a lot about it, Cecil."

"I got a book out of the library because I thought you might be interested to know a bit of background. Like the fact that all the stone to build the Cathedral came from the same quarry at Chilmark."

"What? All of it?"

"Yes."

Cecil went on to tell Noreen more. And more. She curses inwardly the fact that still, all these years later, she is unable to forget the boring aspects of the Cathedral that Cecil could not stop himself telling her about. How the thin stonework of much of the spire is held in place by a cunningly contrived timber scaffolding within the spire, of which more than a third is still of the original wood. Not forgetting that iron brackets fitted to the capstone permit the spire to be 'tightened up' when necessary.

Noreen notices there is an apple on Cecil's locker today. This usually means members of the Saint Vincent de Paul Society have been in to visit him.

"Did you have visitors after I'd gone, yesterday evening, darling?"

Cecil looks up warily. Frowns.

"Visitors? No... no visitors."

Noreen knows that their son, Sean, visited during the evening because he rang her later and told her so. But Sean does not leave apples. Only the Saint Vincent de Paul Society does this. Sometimes it is apples. Sometimes bananas. Sometimes oranges. Once an orange and a pear. They remain on Cecil's locker like nameless calling cards, becoming more and more over-ripe until eventually the staff remove them. Cecil does not like it when they take the fruit away, even though the dried out pips would send out shoots and take root in the top of his locker before he would ever eat it. Noreen knows it is the change he does not like. He usually enjoys the visits and knows the visitors' faces, even if he forgets their names. The visitors from the Saint Vincent de Paul see that the fruit has gone by the time their next weekly visit comes around, and leave more. Noreen knows that it does not matter. That

Cecil is getting a good diet. That the Saint Vincent de Paul Society would feel it enough that Cecil accepts the fruit as a conventional gesture of goodwill.

"But Sean called in, didn't he?"

"Oh, ah, ye'm."

Noreen gets the impression that Cecil does not really remember. Just agrees because he knows that Sean and she are in touch.

"How was he?"

"Oh, just fine, I think."

Sometimes Noreen feels the need to talk to the Matron about Cecil. Like today. Sean had said Cecil had been a bit distracted the previous evening. As if he was keen to get on with things on his own, and yet there was nothing for him to do, except stare blankly at the TV.

The Matron tells Noreen that Cecil is fine. She reminds her it is perfectly normal for people's memory to be a bit less sharp as they grow older. She says he seems quite happy. Always smiling at people and no trouble at all. Spends a lot of time doing his reading and tidying his papers and getting much better at managing his wheelchair.

"One of nature's gentlemen. All the staff say so, Mrs Connolly."

Noreen is reassured. She is tired. It has been a more difficult day than usual. She leaves Cecil early. Drives to Omar's Spar shop at Insole. She often drives there when she feels a bit low. Buys a packet of bread sauce mix. Or Knorr chicken stock cubes. Today, it's Paxo stuffing. Always handy to have in.

FOR A WHILE after Noreen leaves, Cecil tries to remember seeing Sean the previous evening. It is no use. He gets stuck on memories of taking Sean for walks in Llandaff Fields, when Sean was a boy.

Later, of course, things had not been so easy. When Sean was sixteen, he had discovered that there were five public houses in Llandaff – The Mitre, The Heathcock, The Maltsters, The Black Lion and The Butchers. It had seemed to Cecil that on any one evening for the next eight years, if Sean was not in one, he was in another. Cecil could not understand why Sean was so keen to go into pubs every night, instead of inviting friends to the house for a cup of tea. 'I am afraid looking at the world through the bottom of a glass will get him nowhere,' Cecil had repeated to himself, whenever he detected alcohol on Sean's breath. He had worried enormously about the stories Sean told so proudly, after his evenings out; stories which invariably made it sound as if he had been on some wonderful adventure. Drinking with his school-friend Witold, and David, the blind piano tuner. In The Mitre, where they frequently indulged in rough cider and stout, poor man's black velvet. Sean had explained to them with enthusiasm how he had proved beyond doubt that this particular drink got you drunk far more quickly than anything else, information Cecil and Noreen had neither needed nor wanted to hear. Then, at closing time, how they would all retire to Witold's tiny cottage on the banks of the Taff, to sample Polish vodka. One hundred per cent proof, Witold had told Sean. The purest vodka in the world, which, Witold maintained, was actually good for you and could be reactivated the following morning simply by ingesting a little water without food.

Sean had been so keen to be one of the lads, Cecil thought sadly. But sometimes with his other friends, after drinking, he was intolerable, yahooing about outside the house on Marlborough Hill, singing rugby songs, laughing, urinating in the lane, oblivious to the sensibilities of the neighbours.

He turns to something more concrete. The other letter which Noreen wrote to him in September, 1938. For some reason the two September letters have found their way into the same envelope, even though this one was sent two weeks after the other one. Cecil decides that as they are in the same envelope they should count as only one and he will allow himself another letter, later on.

St. Gildas' Convent,
Chard.
Tuesday, September 27th, 1938.

My Dearest Cecil,

I was so impatient to have your latest letter, and so glad when it came this morning. Last night I was wishing the time would fly so that it would soon be morning and I would hear from you and then this morning I began to think that after all you might not write until later in the week, so that I had no peace of mind until I saw the formal and familiar envelope on the table! All of which makes me think how terribly unkind I was during the holidays, when I neglected you for so long. I am still reproving myself.

Thank you for the driving licence – I am not likely to need it again for some time. I did NOT drive in Mr and Mrs Cross's car on Sunday because at the last minute I got 'cold feet' so Margaret had her turn first and though she drives no better than I do – with kangaroo starts, faulty gear changing, etc. – yet she drives STEADILY.

For the first half-hour she kept a steady ten miles per hour uphill and downhill, and at no time did she exceed twenty miles per hour, and even then Mrs Cross was clearly intensely nervous. I knew that it was a physical impossibility for me to drive in so subdued and dignified a manner and the thought of having Mr Cross to superintend scared me to a frazzle, so I gracefully declined on the grounds that I was not so competent as Margaret and so dare not take over.

However I was glad we were going so slowly as I had much to occupy me. They left me in charge of the expedition as they did not know the roads, so I was left to choose a suitable one for a driving lesson. I set us on a course towards Cricket St Thomas, on the Crewkerne road – the familiar turn to the right, then the big bend to the left, (taken in third, and very slowly) and so on down to Broadwindsor, where I saw the telephone box (sorry, kiosk) which once carried our dulcet tones to and from Cornwall on that very memorable day when you were staying down in Lostwithiel and we said we loved each other for the first time. Perhaps we had been too bashful to say it outright to each other in person before? So I had a lot to thank that telephone kiosk for.

It was lovely and yet sad to be going along those roads with anyone but you. I only realised then how many memories we have attached to that neighbourhood. Fortunately, Mrs Cross is a great talker so that I was not given a chance or expected to do more than murmur suitable monosyllables, so I could enjoy all my 'thinks' deep down inside me while her conversation dripped over the surface of my mind. She is quite interesting and amusing, nonetheless. Do you know, she had met this lady from Highbridge who had been living in the typhoid area? She gave us all a really lurid description of the epidemic (I don't know how Margaret managed to keep driving) and some really interesting details; it seems Highbridge men had to take their own glasses if they wanted to drink beer at 'the local', and their money was disinfected by the shopkeepers.

I seem to be easily distracted these days and unable to concentrate on anything properly at the moment. I was flicking through some magazines today and found a birthday fortune book in one of them. I cannot resist passing on some of the best bits about those born between March 22nd and April 20th. Did you know you were born under the sign of Aries, the Ram, a most unprepossessing and pugnacious beast, and consequently you are restless, ambitious, headstrong, practical, original and a 'go-getter'? Apparently, you also make a good organiser and are capable of producing original ideas. BUT Aries people are bad correspondents – their letters are so curt they often cause offence unintentionally (Beware, oh mine Aries, BEWARE!! – but today's was fine!) In matters of love Aries men and women are very rigid and conventional – indeed! Finally, business which suits them is that in which the habit of making decisions quickly is appreciated – Oh, and lots more drivel. I wonder how much of what your stars tell is true. Mine fitted in with me rather well.

Anyway, enough of that. I think it's all because I am just marking time waiting to see what the weekend will bring. Please God there will be no war, but the outlook at the moment is not very cheering. A year ago I would have felt it seriously enough but now the whole question means so much more to me because of you. I find myself wondering only how it will affect you and in thinking that I realise how greatly it will affect everybody, for almost everyone has someone rather precious who would probably have to go. It is a vexed and difficult question, and one can only pray, and even then one realises that God's hands are to a certain extent tied by the hardness and stupidity of man who deliberately casts him aside, despises his grace and follows his own promptings.

I often think how simple life would be if we all just kept those two greatest commandments about loving God above everything and our neighbour as ourselves for God's sake; if we all did this, war and hatred and unkindness would be impossible. But I suppose the devil sees to it that that will not happen. However if our prayers are strong and fervent enough God will help us; and whatever happens we must be ready to accept His will, after all he does know best and, in spite of the devil, whatever work is done on earth is His work, since He wills it and can draw good out of everything.

How inadequately I express myself, I do hope you understand what I am trying to say. Don't worry, my love, you will always be under Our Lady's protection, I think she will always look after you well for me. And remember, whatever happens, wherever you are, I am always praying for you and loving you.

This is all very serious and sad but this crisis makes you think these things and somehow, almost without meaning to, I have jumbled them out to you.

Write to me soon please, in spite of your claim that a letter is inadequate, it means a great deal to me. May the time pass swiftly to our next meeting.

All My Love,
Noreen.

Cecil shakes his head. He remembers it well. The uncertainty of it all. His fear that another conflict was coming, on the same scale as the First World War. His earnest dream of a world at peace fading fast.

The deep impression his father's experience made on him comes back to Cecil. He remembers it was not the words spoken about the war – no words were spoken about it, not to him at least. Nor was it the physical effect on Pop Connolly – he had escaped lightly compared to many thousands of others. A bad hernia, caused by pushing great rolls of signal wire around the battlefield under intense fire. He had been honourably discharged on the 22nd February 1918. 'Served with honour and was disabled in the Great War', was recorded on the illuminated scroll he received.

Sapper Connolly, Royal Engineers. Number 126780. The scroll was issued from the Royal Engineers Record Office in Chatham.

It was the mental effect, Cecil recalls. The look on his father's face. Something had happened to him which had turned the world into a place Cecil could not imagine and did not want to know. Perhaps it had been the incessant shell-fire, sudden explosions, bodies blown to bits in front of his eyes. Cecil did not know for sure and never would.

He had not known his father before the war, had not been born, but as he grew older he felt increasingly that his father was empty, empty of a particular kind of spontaneous affection, as if the stuffing had been knocked out of him. Charming, friendly and kind on the surface, Cecil recalls, but frightened and prone to flashes of anger when under pressure of any sort. Difficult to get close to. And drawn to melancholy when drinking the whiskey or the gin. He thinks back to a day when his father gave him a ride on his shoulders. An ordinary day. Just a ride down the garden. It had been when he was quite young and he remembers his father was showing him cows on the other side of the fence at the bottom of the garden. He had not felt safe. He had never felt secure in his father's care and had grown more and more to rely on his Mammy, and on himself. This was how he coped over the years, so that he and Pop became like strangers. And then unfriendly strangers.

It was very sad, Cecil reflects. He remembers how he had wanted to see his father as a hero when he was young. Had got his father to read the backs of his medals... "The Great War for Civilisation 1914-1919", it said on the bronze one, and King George the Fifth's head was on the other shinier one with a Latin inscription and a slightly different date, 1914-1918. He had got Pop to pin the medals on him with their brightly-coloured ribbons and, when very young, had marched around the parlour carrying Pop's discharge papers, importantly, like a gun against his shoulder. Cecil had nagged and nagged to get Pop to read the discharge papers. "Conduct satisfactory... A good office telephonist... Signed, The Commanding Officer..." He had always insisted that Pop read the description of himself in the discharge papers, "Height, five feet eight and three quarters. Eyes, brown. Hair, brown. Complexion, blank." Pop Connolly always laughed when he said, "Complexion, blank," Cecil remembers. One of Pop's little jokes. Took him years to realise it meant the officer had not made any entry against the section marked Complexion. Occasionally Pop used to rattle off his army number, articulating the numbers with a mechanical bite like a burst of machine gun fire. "Number 1-2-6-7-8-0- Sapper Connolly, Sah!.." He said it with a laugh, but it was the laugh of a man who had sometimes had to act more like a machine than a man, in the face of intolerable danger, fighting his natural instinct for self preservation. The good humour had been there, but sometimes in short supply. Pop had never responded to his requests for stories about the war, however hard he pressed him for one. He had simply been unable to tolerate the sense of horror which he experienced, whenever he was reminded of what he had been through.

So the First World War's effect on his father had given Cecil a horror of war, even without knowing in any detail what Pop Connolly had been through. Cecil knew eight million people had been killed and twenty million had been blinded, maimed or otherwise disabled in the Great War for Civilisation; but it was its effect on one man who survived it, his father, which taught him to abhor war and its corrosive effect on the human spirit.

He remembers how much trust he had placed in the League of Nations, how much hope membership of such a civilising agency had given him, yet when push came to shove, there had been nothing to stop Germany leaving and going its own way. How he had felt for Milan Hodza, the Czech Premier. He remembers seeing pictures of crowds in the streets of Prague calling for the Czech military government to take control and defend their country from aggression. The crowds were denouncing France and Britain and what they believed to be their cowardly compromises – their attempts to avoid war at all costs.

Cecil remembers feeling that Hitler was wrong to want the Sudetenland for Germany. But he can still recall the enormous relief he felt when Germany, England, France and Italy, reached agreement in Munich over annexation of the Sudetenland, and war was averted. He remembers being delighted when he read in the newspaper of Mr Chamberlain's famous announcement on his return from Munich, even though he was on his own in the front parlour of his digs in Frome, at the time.

The fear that war might start anytime created a continual fear that you were no longer master of your own destiny. You might have to leave those you loved. You could not live a normal life. Could not plan for the future. Could not say, "Next year, we'll..." Could only say, "If there isn't a war beforehand, we might be able to..." The enormity of what war might be like was simply too horrendous to contemplate. You lived day to day, appreciating each day as it arrived and trying to make the most of it.

Christmas was enjoyed as if it might be the last. Things were happening in Europe in the months beforehand which gave everybody good cause to fear that Hitler was unpredictable. Kristallnacht. A pretty word. A Christmassy word. Until you learned it was about breaking windows and property belonging to Jews. Somehow one still felt there was something distant, unreal, about it all. It did not affect us. We did not want it to affect us.

Cecil feels thirsty. He reaches for the glass of water beside him. In the rush to try on his new cardigan and to get down to Mass, he realises, he did not take much fluid in. He is hungry too. Must have skimped on breakfast, he thinks. There is an apple on his locker. He decides someone must have left it behind by mistake, perhaps one of the cleaners, and rather than eat it, he determines to wait for whatever meal is next to satisfy his hunger. He has a letter from Noreen to hand, underneath the September envelope.

St Gildas' Convent,
Chard.
December 16th, 1938.

My Very Dearest

I really did not think that I should be able to write to you before leaving Chard, but now I have practically all my packing done and even though I am now sitting in severe and awful silence at my desk in the Senior Class, I have really nothing to do – marks are added, the children are hard at work doing Simple Interest and all I do is occasionally pop around to see if their answers are right. All of which makes me feel extraordinarily 'queer' after working at such high pressure. Looking at them now makes me feel terribly glad I am not at school – it is much nicer to be 'grown-up', able to write a letter instead of doing Simple Interest, to be going home today and in love with the nicest person in the world!

In fact, at the moment, I feel well pleased with life (the only snag being that by tonight I shall be a long way from you – you, of course, would know the actual mileage!) but I was only thinking this morning that, even though it interferes with my private life, all this hard work is worthwhile. It is nice to feel that at the end of a certain time you have achieved something, left your mark, as it were, on people and the place. Firstly, you must rejoice with me that all my infants passed their Music Exam., thank God. I have to thank you, too, as I am sure your Hail Marys helped quite a lot. Then, too, the concert was quite a success, at least everybody said so – actually, I think I am too exacting, I am never perfectly satisfied with what I achieve, I suppose because it could always be better.

Anyhow, everyone else was very pleased and there were no terrible hitches anywhere. The hall was quite crowded – over two hundred there – I should never have thought it would hold so many. Margaret did wonders with the lights, and I looked very nice even if I do say so myself!

I thought afterwards you have never seen me really 'dressed up' – a pity! Still you will have opportunities, no doubt.

I do not know whether to tell you the next bit, but it tickled me tremendously, so I must – Stanley had mentioned something about a dance, one night when we were practising, but I staved him off. And don't say you don't know who Stanley is! He's the peripatetic man who comes in to teach the girls the violin. Remember him now? Anyway, after the concert he asked me again if I would go. I endeavoured to do some more staving, and said I was not dressed for a dance and HE said I looked too nice to dance with!! What do you think of that for a well-turned compliment? I think it is just as well the concert is over or he might develop a real crush. But now I shall not really see him until the next concert two years hence!! All this, of course, is an endeavour to make you green-eyed with jealousy.

NORLAND, 15, Clive Road, Rhosllanerchrugog.

Yes, I am really and truly home – I meant to finish this letter in the train but it was too crowded – I had to get in a carriage with six males, most of them sailors, so I kept my eyes demurely on my book nearly all the time. It was more like being on board ship, the whole train was simply packed with sailors, they were even standing in the corridors. I suppose they were coming on leave from Plymouth.

It now lacks only ten minutes to midnight, so I must hurry to say my goodnight. Daddy has just had to come down to haul Mother and me to bed, poor man knew he would never sleep until we were tucked away for the night. Well, I am sleepy – good night and God bless you – see you in the morning.

SUNDAY.

Well, I am afraid I did not see you in the morning as I stayed in bed late, then Mother came up and talked for ages – five minutes afterwards it was lunch time. Then we talked again and Mrs Howarth, our neighbour, came in to see me. After tea I went out, first to Confession, then to see Clare but she was in Liverpool for the day, only her father at home. Then supper, more talk, bed 11.30pm, so I was too sleepy to write.

However it is now Sunday afternoon, the parents are indulging in 'forty winks' and I am toasting in front of the living room fire. Before I forget, I must tell you, I was laying the table for dinner and put down FOUR places without realising it, we did laugh and, of course, I got teased! I wish I had to lay four places.

I haven't told you yet, have I? I had quite an interesting time before leaving school. First thing in the morning, my exam results, and consequent easing of mind; then a present from Mother Superior of some rather exciting powder and scent, a sort of reward for the Concert; then a delegation of Seniors requesting my presence, upon which I was presented with a rather scrumptious hand-bag and had to try and look as if I enjoyed the little speech and the inevitable 'three cheers' – of course I did not know what to say; then saying goodbye to them in the play-ground and being kissed all over and half-strangled by the little ones; and finally a little crowd of them coming to the station to see me off – à propos of which one of them said, "It's NOT true, you are leaving, is it

Miss Byrne?" Of course, I laughed and said, "No," and then I said, "What did you think I was going to do, if I did not come back?" And they being young and innocent said, "Somebody said you were going to get married."!!! Upon which I laughed more than ever and said of course it was not true and that I would invite them all to the wedding IF ever I did get married – so you won't mind will you?!

I have not been having my deep 'thinks' lately but I have had a very deep longing – for you.

Oh dear, and last night I was wishing and WISHING you could be here for Christmas. Wouldn't it have been too super for words had your mother and father been able to come? You know it really wouldn't have been very difficult. Your people could have gone by train from Chard to Frome and then you could have brought them up here. Then you and your father could have gone back and your mother stayed on a little while – but I suppose it just felt too disruptive an idea, from their point of view.

I shall be left up here all on my own, bored, and pining for you again! The Kolbs want Mother and Father and me to go around to them for Christmas night, but I am not keen and we have not properly decided yet what we shall do.

Incidentally, Mother is not taking very kindly to the idea of my snipping the end off my holiday. She said last night that you had said something about squeezing in a few days at the end, "but...," she went on, "I said to Daddy, I hope Noreen is not thinking of making her holiday here any shorter." I said nothing, it was not a propitious moment!

Yet, all in all, it is so nice now at home. Since your visit, it is "Cecil this..." and "Cecil that..." – you are quite a popular member of the family circle. By the way, I have tried to intimate in various ways to mother that this is the genuine thing and that I regard you as my fate, etc. You know, I think she was slightly surprised – though of course, I said nothing definite, just a few gentle and well-chosen hints. However, she put on a reminiscing air and said, "I don't know, I think girls are foolish to be in a hurry these days. If I had my time over again I would not get married until I was at least thirty." That gives us nine or ten years to wait! Ugh!!

Oh dear! I intended to stop writing a few minutes ago – but I am loathe to leave you, my own. I don't know how you feel? Probably you will tell me that you did not greatly miss me and thought of me, with your own permission, between the hours of 7.30p.m. and 8.00p.m. for the space of three-and-a-half minutes only – oh, sorry, sweetness – I know that is not true – but I MISS you, I WANT you, I do LOVE you.

There, now I am going, so I kiss that very sad-looking face when we said farewell last Sunday and hope that today it is not so sad looking.

Goodbye and God bless you, my darling. All my love,
Noreen.

P.S. I nearly forgot to thank you ever so much for your letter of last Wednesday. It was a great comfort and consolation to me.

N.

Cecil cannot resist reading another letter. There is nobody about. He wants to get through them in good time, before their wedding anniversary later in the month. Reading the letters is taking longer than in previous years, and having to go back and fore in his wheelchair to get them from the box in his locker to read them, or sometimes reading them lying in bed, all adds to the difficulty. He looks back on the letter in which Noreen talks of telling her mother about how she felt about him as the time when he began to believe she was serious about him. Until then, he was sure the bubble would burst; that some fine day Noreen would suddenly realise what he was really like (whatever that was) and she would walk away, politely, smiling, laughing, unreachable evermore. She would not have hurt his feelings. She would just explain what the problem was. In which ways he was not going to be suitable. And walk away. He is unable to imagine how he would have reacted. It does not bear thinking about. He takes the next letter with a sense of relief.

St Gildas' Convent,
Chard.
January 18th, 1939.

My Dearest Cecil,

What a lovely surprise your letter gave me this morning, I have been in a positive GLOW of pleasure since; but profoundly conscious, nevertheless, of my remissness in not having written yesterday. However, I am determined to get something written for you by tonight though I fear it will be scrappy. In fact I am breaking one of my golden rules in writing this – it is during one of my free periods, that I have succeeded in wresting from Mother Superior – however it does not weigh very heavily on my conscience, it is merely poetic justice when one considers how hard I have to work!

It was a great regret to me that you could not make it to our house at Christmas but it has been nicely made up for by my recent visit. By coincidence, with your letter was one from your mother saying she only wishes it had been possible for me to stay on for an extra day or two as she enjoyed my company so much, which I thought very sweet of her.

On Sunday, I went up to the Misses Balcombe for tea and supper. The farm is beautiful but, my love, I am quite positive you would not really like the country – permanently anyhow. It is alright when you are nice and cosy inside (though I imagine your fastidiousness would revolt against smelly oil lamps) but at night outside it is so utterly desolate and so uncomfortably DARK – puddles, mud and unexpected bushes occur at regular intervals of three yards.

However I enjoyed it quite well when I was there. One little bit I enjoyed particularly. I had forgotten to post mother's letter and, since I was at Buckland St Mary, I decided to post it from there. I went down to the village to post it and it was great fun. There was not a soul about and the wind and rain were at their height and I had to battle with them all the way there and back. It was a lovely feeling having the whole world to myself and warring with the elements – that sounds a contradiction doesn't it, but I liked it just for that once, though perhaps repetition would make that sort of thing just a drudge?

I was so wishing I could have had you to talk to on Monday night to give you all my first impressions of the Chard Amateur Dramatic Society – they are really too lengthy and too subtle to write. However – I enjoyed it awfully well and everyone was very sociable, which was really more than I expected. There were one or two people I knew – Marjorie Halse, Jack Aplin, Joan Major and Mr. Rabley. Then there was Saunders, the Chemist chap. I could not stand the sight of him in the shop, he was so abrupt, in fact I deserted Saunders' Chemist's shop for Boots on his account. But having met him at the Dramatic I find he is a harmless, friendly sort of chap.

Those are all I knew, and I was introduced to so many that I have forgotten half of them – the producer chap is nice and very capable – in fact they really do the thing awfully well. There are very few weak links. But you know I was thinking afterwards, I am just not used to mixing with non-Catholic company and something about the atmosphere was somehow – well, different. I mean the way the girls sit around in abandoned positions and show an unnecessary amount of leg and the way the fellows casually put their hands on your shoulders as they peer into the middle distance, if they are standing near enough – that sort of thing makes me a bit shuddery and I hope I shall never get used to it. No doubt it is my convent upbringing bearing fruit. Well, I'm going to have to leave it here for the time being, Sister Immaculata is ringing the bell like billyo for changeover of lessons, so that's the end of my free period. Honestly, I don't know where Sister Immaculata gets the energy. Stop! Stop! You're damaging my eardrums, Sister! And yet she looks so frail and is suffering from some mysterious illness which nobody will put a name to.

4.45p.m.

I am back in my room now. The last lesson went quite well. Tonic solfa. Except that little Dobbins, Dobbo – they call her, was fiercely sick just as she was hitting top C. "Doh, ray, me, fah, soh..." Then I moved my pointer to top C. "Doh... ooo...ooo...eee..." She had been looking a little green all lesson. Or it may have been that she was just trying too hard. Anyway she was fine immediately afterwards, once the after-sick formalities were completed. I sent one of the more responsible girls for the caretaker, Mr Mahoney, and he came immediately and spread sawdust over the unfortunate accident (the sick, not poor Dobbo!). Dobbo was despatched to the cloakrooms with her class-mate, Angela Balcombe, another day-girl and a niece of the Balcombes. Dobbins came back far happier after rinsing her face in cold water and responded really well to all the sympathy we gave her.

At the moment, Margaret is in my room and though actually she has spoken precisely five words since she came in about half an hour ago, still I cannot enjoy writing with another presence in the room. Ah, well – nil desperandum!

By the way, Sergeant and Mrs Doughty were not at Mass on Sunday, so it looks as though they are still away. Also I have not seen Mrs Aplin since I came back to Chard, I believe Mrs Day is very ill and she is with her all the time. One thing I noticed the other night at the Dramatic was how wretchedly ill Jack Aplin looked, he is so THIN, his face looks positively emaciated – beside him you are like a Glaxo baby.

Incidentally, I was glad you wrote to mother the other day. I had a letter from Daddy yesterday and, according to 'the latest bulletin', she needs cheering up as she is no better.

She often has 'a chest' at this time of the year, so I expect she will recover soon.

Oh, I nearly forgot... after about an hour's wrestling with an A.B.C. Timetable I discovered some rather uncomfortable times for getting from Chard to Frome the weekend after next. I shall have to leave Chard by 'bus at 8.45a.m. which arrives at Crewkerne at 9.05a.m. The 'bus from Crewkerne to Yeovil departs from Crewkerne at 9.10a.m. (with me on it, so long as the Chard-Crewkerne 'bus arrives on time!). The Crewkerne-Yeovil 'bus arrives in Yeovil at 9.45a.m. and departs for Frome at 9.51a.m., or there is a later 'bus which departs at 11.21a.m. The earlier 'bus arrives in Frome at 10.29a.m. and the later one at 11.59a.m. So you see that, if you cannot get away from work until midday, I shall have to wait about an hour and a half, either in Yeovil or Frome. The next 'bus from Crewkerne would not get me to Yeovil in time for either the 9.51a.m. departure or the 11.21a.m. departure, and the above are the only possible times.

You will note that I have taken a leaf out of your book, with regard to organising my trip.

On balance, I think it would be better for me to wait in Yeovil since I know the place and could find something to do there. I suppose you could not get off at eleven o'clockish, could you? If you could then I should come to Frome for 10.29a.m. Anyhow, let me know about it when you write.

You know, I really don't know whether you should come THIS Sunday? It is such a long way, my angel, and you know I DID say that we ought to cut our meetings down to once a fortnight this term. I mean the other night I had had my supper and played about and then got cosily ensconced in front of the fire when I looked at the clock and thought how you were still on the road driving back to Frome and still had a good way to go.

What a lot I have written – but as mother always says, I write a lot with nothing in it – Oh! before I go, I wrote to Mrs

Port and presented your point of view very sweetly about the whist drives and the need to hold them regularly so that people do not lose interest, I hope she accepts it. At least she is still speaking to me!

I'm sure there was something else I wanted to tell you – but it's gone, as I shall be in a minute. God bless you, my own.

All My Love

Noreen.

P.S. I know now, I am enclosing the poem I spoke about – it seems to say in poetry what you have often said lately.

N.

Cecil is surprised. He is surprised every year by this post script. He knows it refers to the Robert Bridges poem which he so often recites to himself. He holds the copy of it in his hand, written out by Noreen in a particularly neat handwriting, to mark its specialness. *So Sweet Love Seemed.* But he loves her in the same way as he has always loved her. He knows this will never change. He has forgotten the things he said which made Noreen allude to that poem in her postscript. She must have got him wrong in that regard, he is sure.

ა

THE LETTERS are like having Noreen with him. In spirit at least. He remembers most of the experiences they refer to as if they had only taken place a week last Thursday. In fact he remembers them much better than he remembers what happened a week last Thursday. He remembers receiving the letters. He remembers where he was at the time. He remembers how he felt when he read their contents. He remembers what he said to Noreen about some of the things she wrote and what she said to him about things he wrote to her. For some reason she cannot be with him at this hotel. A pity. They are very good here, if one sets to one side their lack of punctuality. The food is always hot. They have Mass on the premises every day. Still, at least Noreen comes to see him every day. Actually, twice a day, he reminds himself. It could be worse. And she is always the same. Full of life. Full of joy. He reaches for his cashbox. Dips his hand in, feels for the next letter.

St Gildas' Convent,
Chard.
Monday, January 23rd, 1939.

My Angel,

I am glad you decided to come over on Saturday, after all – and thank you a thousand times for my birthday present. You ARE clever because it is so lovely and fulfils a long cherished desire of my secret soul. With a writing case as beautiful as this, how will I ever be able to hold anything back? It is all very well your asking me to tell you all my most secret thoughts, but I have an uncanny feeling that you know them anyway!

I remember Margaret used to have a writing case – not half as marvellous as this – and the longing to possess one that used to assail my heart, when I saw her carrying it into the study room to write her letters, was almost unbearable. It is so lovely to have something so scrumptious of your very own – I keep stroking it with a quiet air of pride every time I look at it.

My sweet, you are so good, I DO wish you would not buy me such lovely things.

Incidentally, it was a great surprise. I knew you had an idea that my birthday was somewhere hereabouts but I did not think you knew the exact date and I fondly hoped that you had forgotten all about it – anyway, it is much too soon after Christmas to have a birthday – otherwise, if I had known you knew when it was, I should have issued some stern and timely warnings! But, oh, I do thank you so very, very much.

I have had quite a nice time today – mother sent me some very nice gloves, Daddy a fat box of chocolates, also I had another box of chocolates from one of the girls and a pair of silk stockings off Margaret. Mother also sent me a rain-proof pixie cap, lined with material. She said it would do for the car but I do not know whether I like it, I shall have to keep it until you pass judgement.

Sister Catherine cooked a cake for me and Sister Immaculata put Happy Birthday in green icing on it and, of course, I had lots of cards. But it is rather strange, this year I have barely thought about my birthday, it arrived almost as a shock this morning.

You know, my darling, when I got your present this morning it made me think, somehow (I suppose because my thoughts were particularly tender at that moment), how absolutely essential you are to me. I really feel I COULDN'T do without you now.

Do you realise that you possess me as entirely as it is possible for you to possess me at the present time? You know

I have always made a great confidante of mother, but neither she nor anybody else has ever received my confidence to the extent you have. Another thing, I have never liked the idea of males touching me or kissing me; it always seemed rather repulsive. But with you my feelings have always been quite the contrary, with the exception of only one occasion, and you know when that was. I am afraid that sometimes I give you reason to doubt but, truly, my darling, I do look forward with all my heart to when we shall be really united for the rest of our lives. If that hope and your love were suddenly taken out of my life now, I just cannot imagine what I should do.

You speak of what I have given you but you cannot know what you have given me. Sometimes when I think of your love it makes me hold my breath, mentally and physically, and I could almost weep at my own littleness and my own worthlessness.

If it wasn't for this talk of war all the time, wherever you go and whenever you pick up a newspaper – will there be one, won't there be one? – I think I would be completely happy, or at least as completely happy as I could be without spending every minute of every day in your company. Do you think Pres. Roosevelt spending more on national defence means he's got the wind up – and is preparing for war, without saying so exactly?

Thank you again and pray hard for me, my own, it is not too soon to pray for all the graces we shall both need, not only this year, but next year and all the years to come.

Good night and God bless you.

All my love for always,

Noreen.

Cecil relishes the memory of how he befriended Sister Catherine and Sister Immaculata and thus found out the date of Noreen's birthday. He had found it difficult, keeping to himself the fact that he knew, but it had been worth it. The Sisters had even allowed him into the kitchens to help make the cake, strictly against the rules but Catherine and Immaculata had reached a point in their lives at which Mother Superior's authority meant less to them. Poor old Sister Catherine was even older than Sister Immaculata, practically at death's door, he remembers with a smile, and she needed him to carry the big Pyrex mixing bowl here and there and to lower the completed mix into the oven. They had welcomed the diversion as both the Sisters were retired, apart from Sister Immaculata's job ringing the school bell, and time sometimes hung heavy on their hands.

"You look flushed, C. Are you all right?" Noreen is leaning over Cecil, pressing down heavily on each side of his body, trapping him with his blanket. He wriggles just enough to allow him to draw in the hand holding the letter and conceals it beneath the blanket.

"Mmmm... 'st have nodded off for a moment. Oh, yes. I'm just fine. How about you? Are you alright?"

"Yes, I'm very well. I had a catnap myself, at home, funnily enough."

Ah, Cecil thinks. 'At home'. He had wanted to ask about that. Why Noreen does not come in to live with him here at the hotel. Or himself link up with her again 'at home'. He resolves to ask her when she comes in next. Must have dropped off again. She has gone. Has left him a little note: 'Stayed for half an hour, but you were sleeping like a baby and I didn't have the heart to wake you up. See you tomorrow. All my love. Noreen.'

Cecil replaces the letter he is holding and extracts the next.

St. Gildas' Convent,
Chard.
Sunday, February 5th. 1939.

My Dearest Cecil,

You are a spoilt baby, and yet you infer that I neglect you, (don't forget I traipsed all the way to Frome on the 'bus last weekend, just because you had to work on a Saturday!) but here I am, only thirteen hours after having seen you yesterday, and when I really should be writing home, sitting down to commune with you.

I have just been to Mass and the Reverend Father O'Beirne was in fine form – first of all he said, "The collection last Sunday for the gas bill amounted to sixteen shillings and eight pence halfpenny. The gas bill is twenty six shillings and four pence. Therefore we will have another special collection next week!"

Another thing Father O'Beirne said was that we ought to celebrate Saint Patrick's Day by having a Dance and Social. He said everyone must come and he would be waiting until one day when the Mother Superior was in a good humour and she would probably let us have the Hall – isn't that exciting?

Incidentally, the Doughtys were not at Mass again this morning. I wonder if they have forgotten that the time for Mass has been moved to nine o'clock?

Oh, sweetness, wasn't it lovely yesterday? I did love you so terrifically, did I tell you? I have carefully taken my throat to pieces and examined it for germs labelled C.J.C.; there were, in fact, one or two but I chased them diligently and speared them with a knitting needle! I do hope you do not feel any worse today, and that you got back safely last night. There is one thing that consoles me, it is not so cold today so that if you have to go over to Yeovil with your work you will probably only get pneumonia and not double-pneumonia, as you would have done if it had been like yesterday.

By the way, we got our supper all right when we got in last night, although it was late – and, by the way, Margaret left the pie-dish from our 'Antarctic' picnic in the car, did you break it? I bet you cussed when you found it.

You know, sweetness, I wish that you would repent and give up the idea of coming next Saturday to the play. Noel Coward is not really your cup of tea, is he? I know how you abhor the idea of divorce and 'Private Lives' is about two disastrous second marriages! Honestly, I should mind terribly if you are in the audience, it would be a sort of nightmare that would pursue me all week – when I am with you and you look at me like you do, and say things in that wheedling tone I feel that I can't say no, but when I am away from you I know how I should hate it – "Please!" (with a very beseeching look).

And now I really must fulfil my filial obligations and write home, so regretfully I leave you. Thank you again for the lovely day yesterday, it really was so nice.

Darling, you WILL tell me, won't you, just exactly how your cold is; it is quite a bad one, you know, and you did look wonky yesterday, and I can't help feeling a bit worried, especially as it will be my fault if it gets any worse.

À bientôt, chéri, and please write soon, because I feel so awfully lonely for you. I kiss you oh, so very, very tenderly and lovingly and gently and tell you that I am,

Your very own,
Noreen.

Cecil turns over, facing the wall. If he closes his eyes he can see Noreen in her costume, a short black dress, playing in *Private Lives*. It was the first time he had seen her on the stage. He disapproved of the play's plot and Noreen twirling a two foot long cigarette holder between her fingers – and smoking. But he was captivated by her performance. When he wakes, he wants to read more.

St. Gildas' Convent,
Chard.
Wednesday, 22nd February, 1939.

My Dearest One,

I suppose you were half-expecting a letter from me this morning and I did intend to write last night but AFTER I had dealt with some of my neglected correspondence, however the task was so formidable that there was no time to write to you after all. I still have about four letters to write but I thought I had better begin with you this morning – oh, blow, I mean this evening. It's a perfectly foul evening, wind, rain and cold, not very promising for the weekend – because I AM coming, please God.

I feel lots better, in fact almost quite better. Do you know what I thought the other night, wouldn't it be fun if we could go and dance somewhere on Saturday night? It is going to be ages before the much-heralded Saint Patrick's Day Dance in the Convent Hall, and that may prove to be a fairly staid affair in any case. Of course, it is unlikely that there will be any hops as it is Lent, but should I bring a glad rag, in case? I know the idea will not appeal to you, but it would blow away a few cobwebs for me and would be an opportunity for doing together one of the things we miss.

One of the letters I wrote last night was to Mrs Port as I had a card from her yesterday morning desiring your Frome address – so expect to hear from her or to receive a visit! It is a good job I know she is a respectably married woman. Such goings on... are you sure it is just your mutual interest in whist drives which brings you together so often!..

Darling, talk about loving people, I loved you terrifically on Sunday night. You know you were so patient and sweet with me all day. Thank you so much for being so nice, I am afraid that sometimes my tongue is a little sharp and I don't always bother stopping myself saying things I shouldn't – but that must be my Lenten penance. You are not in the least 'wooden'. Stoical in expression perhaps, but 'wooden' no. I think I was perhaps still a little high after all the excitement of the play the evening before. I am so glad you enjoyed it, despite all my previous forebodings.

I wonder if you would excuse me now and let me off with this scrappy letter for I have several things to do and not much time to do them in as we are having Benediction this evening. It is one of those occasions when Mother Superior likes all the pupils who can to be present and ditto the teachers, even though it is out of school hours.

So goodbye and God bless you, my dearest one.

All My Love,

Noreen.

The following Saturday was when Cecil proposed to Noreen. Cecil had not planned it in advance. He remembers how for several months he and Noreen had fallen into the habit of talking as if their eventual marriage was taken as read. They had made clear to each other how serious their intentions were, how neither could envisage life without the other and how, naturally, that meant they wanted to spend the rest of their lives together. Eventually, it had dawned on Cecil that he had not formally popped the question. Somewhat remiss of me, he chastises himself sleepily; but he explains to himself he was young and finding his way in a situation which was new to him. He had a notion that the proposal should be made in a romantic ambience. And in a way which Noreen would remember for the rest of her life. It was essential she should say 'yes', after all. He did not want to get it wrong, end up antagonising or upsetting Noreen.

Cecil had the idea of weaving into his proposal a reference to the legend of King Arthur. He felt this would give the moment a kind of dignity and drama which the bald enquiry, "Will you marry me?" would lack. Cecil had already half-framed in his mind the words he would use, several weeks before... "Lady Noreen, will you do me the huge honour of marrying me and living forevermore in the castle of our love?" The Arthurian link was to derive mainly from the setting. About two years previously Cecil had visited Dozmary Pool on Bodmin Moor, where legend suggests that an arm once emerged from the waters to receive the sword Excalibur and draw it down into the depths of the lake.

Noreen had arrived in Frome that weekend desperately keen that they should find a dance to go to. With Cecil's landlady's permission, Noreen had popped up to his room to change into her evening dress and when she came back downstairs she looked as beautiful as Cecil had ever seen her. She did not often use make-up but on this occasion, perhaps because she was away from the confines of the Convent in Chard, she had used a delicate touch of powder and a bright red lipstick.

As they set out into town, Cecil had realised that he should have made enquiries about dances in advance. It was not like him to overlook such a basic need. Perhaps his lack of aptitude for dancing had played a part in this oversight, he thinks with the benefit of hindsight. He and Noreen had driven around Frome once or twice and not found any dances going on anywhere. Cecil, keen to prevent Noreen's growing disappointment from turning to disillusionment, had suddenly said, "I know what I'll do, I'll take you on a mystery tour." In his mind's eye, he could see Dozmary Pool on a bright June day – but this was the middle of winter.

Their journey in the direction of Dozmary Pool went quite well until they reached Okehampton. Thus far, Noreen had risen magnificently to the occasion, maintaining a lively sense of expectation over where their mystery destination might be. However, it had been quite dark when they set out from Frome. It was a cold evening with frost setting on the ground. And Noreen was wearing only a thin coat over her dress. Cecil had wanted to show Noreen a bit of Okehampton, as it was on their route, and, whilst they were driving around, Noreen spotted the Plymouth Inn. She had expressed a huge enthusiasm to go in. Cecil had wanted to press on, at least to Launceston, but he concurred and said, "Just for a few minutes, then."

Once inside, Noreen had been fascinated by the fact that the Plymouth was an old coaching inn, and then she had become involved in a series of games of shove ha'penny with some of the regulars, and followed that up with several games of darts. The warmer she got, the less she showed any interest in going any further on their mystery tour. Cecil recalls that he then made one of those quick decisions which Noreen had told him Ariens were capable of. He manoeuvred Noreen to a wooden settle near the fire, away from the bar games, and he spoke quietly to her, "This is the end of the mystery tour, Noreen. Here at Okehampton. Listen. Listen, a minute. Lady Noreen, will you do me the honour of marrying me, and..."

"Yes... Oh, yes, yes, a thousand times, yes..." she had whispered back.

The relief had been instantaneous. As Noreen's arms had encircled Cecil's neck and her lips met his, he had been acutely aware of salty tears in the corners of his eyes.

Cecil remembers how Noreen had cut in with her acceptance of his proposal, before he had quite finished his piece. But it had not mattered. Not in the least. And she had been wonderful about the ring, which he had still to buy. They had bought it the following weekend, when they drove up to Rhosllanerchrugog so that Cecil could ask Jack Byrne for his daughter's hand in marriage. They had driven across to Wilks, the Wrexham jewellers, and found the perfect ring. Three diamonds. An eighteen carat gold band. It had fitted straight away.

The meeting with Jack Byrne had gone well but had

been somewhat less euphoric. Jack had directed Cecil into the living room, upon his asking to speak to him in private and had shown no sense of urgency. He had pulled up two battered old chairs beside the fire. Cecil remembers he had wanted to get the meeting over with. Cecil had not anticipated any possibility that Jack Byrne would seek to withhold his consent to their marriage.

"Mr Byrne, I would like to ask..."

Jack Byrne had held a large hand up imperiously, palm-outward.

"Stop, young man. Let's do this properly, shall we?" Jack had said, reaching for two bottles of Guinness off the sideboard, with his other hand. With great deliberation, he had poured the stout into glasses. He had stood the glasses in the hearth to let the froth settle, then carefully selected the poker from the stand, where it dangled alongside the hearth brush and the coal tongs, and pushed the blackened end into the foot of the fire.

"Let's take a whet together, shall we?" Upon saying this, Jack Byrne had reached for his pipe and matches and begun to gulp great mouthfuls of smoke, in and out like a bellows, to get the pipe burning.

"Thank you," Cecil had said. Cecil remembers thinking how he had expected their meeting to be brief, business-like and tinged with gratitude on Jack's part that so worthy a young man had chosen Noreen. As the minutes had passed, however, he had begun to wonder if what he had to ask might not be regarded so favourably as he had assumed it would be, or if not that, at least his seeking of permission was going to be something of an anti-climax, after such a lengthy build up in response to his simple request for a few words in private.

Jack Byrne had waited until he adjudged the poker to be hot enough and had then thrust it into each of the glasses of Guinness. For a moment, Cecil had entertained the crazy notion that for two pins Jack would have happily thrust the poker into each of his eyes. He was certain that Jack knew what he wanted to ask him and that this unnecessary charade was meant to impress upon him Jack Byrne's importance, and that Jack's wishes now, and in the future, should not be lightly ignored. But, fortunately, that fancy had soon passed and Cecil had found himself smiling gratefully at Jack as he handed him a steaming Guinness.

"Sláinte," Jack had said.

"Cheers," he had replied.

That had seemed to break the ice. Cecil had soon found himself asking for Noreen's hand in marriage and extolling her sterling virtues to her father in an open and sincere fashion, even if still a little nervously. Jack Byrne had listened with a serious expression on his face and then grasped Cecil's hand in his.

"Son," he had said. No more. No less. Cecil could not have asked for more.

As he grasps his counterpane with his own pale white hand, Cecil can still picture Jack Byrne's big hand, his huge red fingers like uncooked sausages. Can still feel his warm, vice-like grip.

CECIL WAKES with a dry mouth and indigestion. It is the early hours of Saturday morning. At least, he thinks it is the early hours of Saturday morning. He has noticed that they serve fish every Friday in this hotel and smoked haddock has a tendency to give him indigestion. Always has done. He is pretty sure that haddock was served for dinner last evening. Recalls struggling a bit with the bones and having to leave a lot of it.

So he stares around his room. The light is on all night. Never usually troubles him because he is asleep. He cannot get into the wheelchair to turn it off. Not without help from the night porter, if there is one. Has no phone beside the bed, cannot summon the porter even if they do have one. Resigns himself to the fact that getting back to sleep is going to be difficult. He stretches his arm out as far as his locker and tugs it toward him. Extracts his cashbox. His letters. The ones from February 1939 are out of their envelopes. Read them yesterday. He takes the next one. March 23rd, 1939. He ponders over what might have happened during the first three weeks of March. He has absolutely no recollection whatsoever. They would have been working hard during the day. Managed to see each other at weekends? No need to write? Hard to say. Maybe Noreen will remember. Probably not. He will ask her when he sees her.

Anyway he has the letters. He always rejoices in his own foresight and wisdom in deciding to keep Noreen's letters and the other papers, his treasures, keepsakes, touchstones. They bring back so much which otherwise would be lost to him, memories which have always

119

sustained him; those memories which could otherwise have dissolved like sea-mist on a sunny morning if they had been thrown away, he thinks. That was good, he smiles to himself. Would have dissolved like sea-mist on a sunny morning. Noreen would have liked to hear me think that. She likes it when I am imaginative. Anyway.

St. Gildas' Convent,
Chard.
23rd March, 1939.

My Dearest Love,

Your letter this morning was like an oasis in the desert; I feel considerably refreshed by it. Of course, it was the handwriting, the familiar style and signature which provided this refreshment. The actual subject matter caused me to cast mine eyes heavenwards with an imploring expression signifying, "Is it to be always thus, O Lord, always thus?" However, since it seems it must be always thus that I should be bullied, overridden and over-ruled – behold me, subjected and obedient, ready to travel to the ends of the earth in answer to your lightest whim. To whit, I shall be ready at 1.30p.m. on Saturday.

Actually, I was not surprised since I had received a letter from your mother on Tuesday in which she warned me that your father was writing to you inviting you and me to visit them and suggesting that you wrote to ask me. Your mother's letter said, "No excuses accepted, under any circumstances, please..." – What an insistent family! Still, kind of them to include me.

So now I shall have to contrive and devise examination papers in half the time I was allowing myself – still, I'm sure I'll manage it.

What about Poland? You don't think Hitler would chance his luck there too, do you? Anyway, it looks as if we could be dragged in, if he is ever that foolish. What do you think? Am

I worrying overmuch?

> Au revoir, mon cher,
> Lots of love,
> *Noreen.*

Cecil thinks back gratefully to his mother's intervention. She had encouraged his father to write to him so that there would be a chance for them all to spend time together and get to know each other properly. They had enjoyed a happy weekend in a wooden holiday chalet in Lostwithiel. All had been on their best behaviour. Even he and his father had made an effort, buoyed up by Noreen's effervescence and Mammy's patient good humour. They had cooked a lovely Sunday dinner together before leaving. A huge joint of beef, with roast potatoes, carrots, peas and gravy. Noreen and Mammy had managed this together, without one cross word. Noreen had been careful not to interfere in Mammy's arrangements and continually asked her what she wanted her to do and how she would like things done. This worked exceedingly well. By the end of the weekend Cecil could see Pop and Mammy approved of his choice, that was the main thing. In fact, he began to experience a slight feeling of irritation towards his father who began to get very matey with Noreen over the subject of horseriding, a topic Pop Connolly knew little of, apart from at one remove through his interest in horse-racing.

There had been just the one letter in March. None in April. The more we were seeing each other, the less we needed to write, of course, Cecil reminds himself sadly.

> *St. Gildas' Convent,*
> *Chard.*
> *Sunday May 7th, 1939.*

My Dearest Cecil,

Here I am again, addressing you from my bed, and in much more sober mood than last week although there have been one or two funny moments. I feel as though I have dozens of things to tell you although there is only one thing of real interest which I shall tell you anon.

I have had a desperately busy day: Up this morning at 7.15a.m., breakfast and Mass. Breakfast was over by 7.45a.m., two rounds of toast oozing with butter and apricot jam, piping hot coffee and a chat with Sister Maria, then in for the early Mass at the Church of the English Martyrs, where I totally disgraced myself at the collection! As Mr Cross went up the aisle with the collection plate, I discovered I did not have my handbag. I leaned forward to ask Margaret if she could lend me sixpence but half way through my trying to explain what I wanted, for some unknown reason, we both burst out laughing and I could not go on. There I was in hysterics, wondering if she had understood and incapable of further explanation. However, just as Mr Cross collected the first ha'penny from one of the boarders in the front bench, Margaret passed sixpence back to me and I was saved.

After Mass, I wrote home and managed another letter to my friend Clare Kolb and the weather was so nice that I took my armchair out beside the fire escape where a tragedy very nearly occurred. My beautiful blue writing case was lying open on a small chair near me when a most ill-mannered bird took a great liberty with a piece of this note paper which happened to be lying on top of the other things inside the case. Fortunately the case was open and the note paper sustained the only damage – a timely warning not to use it outside again.

After dinner, I went for a short walk with a few of the girls and Sister Maria with whom I had a very spiritual talk. I was only thinking afterwards how little you have the opportunity for anything like that. It is so lovely to hear a really good, pure, holy soul talking, and she is not in the least preachy;

but it is nice how everyone here talks so easily and naturally of things spiritual.

After the walk, I WORKED – from about 2.45p.m.-4.00p.m. and then from about 5.00p.m.-6.20p.m. and again after supper until about 9.30p.m. I was sort of hurrying all the time in case you would be coming and I think in hurrying so much it took me longer because I kept thinking of why I was hurrying and consequently of you, so that there were frequent intervals of acute distraction. After supper Mother Superior came to me with a funny little face and said, "Do you know the latest news? Father O'Beirne wants to hold another garden fête in the summer in aid of the school!" I nearly passed out, but it seems he communicates with Mother Superior from time to time and the latter is undoubtedly keen on the idea. It seems at first Mother Superior said 'no', perhaps influenced by the poor turnout for the Saint Patrick's Day Dance fiasco (Did I remember to tell you about that? Crates and crates of Guinness and no outside people. Father O'Beirne ended up drinking most of it himself and poor Sister Immaculata got quite tiddly). Anyway, Father O'Beirne pressed the point saying how some of the money could go towards the Playground Fund (it desperately needs resurfacing, it is so badly rutted over at least half its surface) and how he would shoulder most of the responsibility for organising it, etc., so she has more or less agreed. I shan't like it a bit because it won't be YOUR garden fête and I don't think I shall be able to stand it. However, there it is, what do you think of the idea?

Incidentally, it is very unofficial yet, but of course as usual I long to tell you everything the minute I hear it.

Oh dear, for about three minutes then there was a big pause while I said goodnight to you in my imagination – it was such a nice one, please imagine it nicely. Do you know that you are in my thoughts from the first instant I wake until I sleep again at night. Now I MUST leave you.

Goodnight and God Bless you, my darling,
Noreen.

*

Cecil knows that, for others, the weather always seems to have been warmer, the summers longer, in their youth. He is not sure if this is so in his case. He never recalls having felt the heat very greatly, not being prone to give way to an impulse to run very frequently, except when under extreme duress of some sort, as when having to run for a bus during the years when he did not own a car, though he had been known to walk briskly when his spirits were high, which was often, and when he was on some errand of importance.

He has always noticed the weather, however, and its effect on one's life. But perhaps never for a particularly lengthy period of time. A perfunctory glance has usually sufficed when gauging if a coat would be needed outdoors or not. As Cecil gets into his next letter, however, he cannot help recognising that the turning of the seasons, rather than the outdoor temperature or sunniness as such, perhaps had a stronger effect on him when younger than he is now aware. Or it may just be the effect Noreen's letter has upon him. He can see the beautiful grounds of St Gildas' Convent again, experience the stillness of a spring evening. It is the month of May, in Chard.

St. Gildas' Convent,
Chard.
Monday 22nd May, 1939.

My Very Dearest,

I have just come in from a fairly vigorous game of tennis; it is too dark to play any longer and it is too light to go to bed or to switch on my bed-side lamp.

Margaret has gone to bed and now, though it is only 9.20p.m., an unbroken silence pervades the house. It is rather a lovely time the evening I think, there is a mellowness and calm about it that you never get with the morning.

Really, I do wish you could see out of my window with me now. There is a background of thick green trees and a lovely evening sky. Over in the orchard the trees are snowy with blossom and, just on either side of Our Lady's statue, I can see two yellow tulips that look just like two burning lamps. The gym-room windows are closed and give it such a fast-asleep air and behind it is a very tall tree like a sentinel. Judy, the cow, is in the field looking ever so wise and content and I can see a black, sinuous body moving swiftly through the laurel bushes. Even as I have been writing the last birds have twittered good night and I can just imagine them lying so cosy and snug in their nests. Have you ever watched a bird closing its eyes to go to sleep? It looks so sweet and helpless.

You know I often want you most at this time, the sort of 'resting time' before going to bed. It is so comforting to have someone to tell your thoughts to and somehow I always feel that this time is made for confidences and close companionship.

Last night when I was in bed thinking of us I had a very sudden and strong conviction that a holiday 'en famille' in September would not be much good – I mean, FUN. Darling, let's go by ourselves somewhere, in August. We've never been really by ourselves to do what we liked, when we liked, how we liked, have we? I mean there has always been a family knocking around whenever we have had any length of time together. I think I could coax Mother around to not finding it too shocking and then our united persuasions could convert Daddy. But I do want it so awfully and I know you do. I mean if you just let your imagination run on and see the two of us lazying about in some forsaken and exquisite spot beside the sea (I put us in Anglesey, for some reason) and having such FUN together and oh! – everything, is simply irresistible, isn't it? After all you could have a holiday with your people in September.

But, oh dear, I have remembered probably you could not get any leave in August and have already booked two weeks in September, probably it's quite impossible – oh blow! I wish I had never thought of it. That's the worst of having an imagination.

Time I went to bed now, my sweet. Good night and God Bless.

X.

TUESDAY

All hail, my beloved, – prepare for an anti-climax for you behold no longer a being who rhapsodizes over evening trees and evening skies but a being who clings to the bed-post to stop the world from slipping away from her, a being who has breakfasted on a square inch of dry toast and been violently sick – in fact a being in the throes of a bilious attack. Such is life with its bodily frailties mocking our little minds.

Well, since writing is somewhat difficult, I must needs say goodbye until a more auspicious moment.

Oh for the touch of your gentle hands to soothe my wracked head.

Keep well, my love, until I see you again.

Goodbye, my own,

Noreen.

Cecil's left arm has gone numb. He has been leaning on his left side and holding the letter in his left hand. He takes a minute to massage some life back into his arm.

He used to feel so helpless in Frome, he recalls. Forty miles away from Chard, the town he knew best, the town where his parents were living, and the town where Noreen had to live aching to spend every minute with him, yet trapped there by force of circumstances. He had gone through agonies of indecision. Should he go back to Chard? Get a job in the Post Office again? Give up his career ambitions? Noreen meant everything to him. Yet again there was the uncertainty over whether there was going to be a war and whether that might mean he would be needed to enter a theatre of war on behalf of his country anywhere in the world, which he was perfectly willing to do so long as war was unavoidable. He could only take each day as it came and do his best that day. There was no point in doing something hasty. It would have served no purpose. They had each other. They had become engaged.

At first they had kept the fact of their engagement in the family. They had been concerned that making it public would put pressure on them – to set a date for a wedding, to tell others their plans, where they would be living, when Noreen would be leaving her job and moving away from Chard – if she was going to be moving away, whether Cecil's parents would be moving to be closer to Cecil and Noreen once they had set up home together and so that Cecil's mother could be on hand if they started their family off in the near future. All this when they were uncertain themselves over the answers to many of the questions.

As time went on they had shared the fact of their engagement with people outside the immediate circle of their families. When they had felt a bit more secure about some of the answers to the main questions people might ask, they had chosen in whom they would confide very carefully. It had felt like protecting a state secret at times. As he reads the next letter, Cecil remembers that it was not until June that Noreen decided to wear her engagement ring in public.

St Gildas' Convent,
Chard.
June 4th, 1939.

My Dearest and Best Beloved One,

Oh, dear! I am so terrifically lonely for you, I have been positively miserable all afternoon because I find it so hard being without you. I want nothing except to run into your arms and lie there quite quietly without saying a word or thinking a thought, and you would be in one of your nice moods and not ask me what I was thinking about but would just love me and love me. – Oh blow! I must not start letting myself go on like this, it is a lack of self-control, but I DO want you.

Yes, thank you, in reply to the question you ask in your letter, I AM feeling full of beans physically, probably because I had a good night's sleep when I came back yesterday night. I have started to break the news of our engagement here; I started with Mother Superior – she was very gracious in congratulating me and sent her best wishes to you of course, but I could not help being just a trifle disappointed in her response. She was somehow 'cold' about it, hard to describe it really, I don't think I can deal with it adequately in a letter. Everyone else responded more or less as you would expect them too. Margaret said she had been sure we were engaged for ages but had not liked to be so rude as to ask me outright whether we were or not!

Last evening I went up town and met Mrs Southwood. She stopped to talk and I kept my hand discreetly at my side but a lady was with her and she stood away from us in full view of my left hand. I have a feeling it was Mrs Young, you know, Mrs Cross's friend – she was dark and stout with glasses. She looked at me very fixedly all the time, so I strongly suspect that the cat is well and truly out of the bag.

I had a very long and interesting talk with Father O'Beirne last night. He is something of a revelation when one gets to know him. He spoke very calmly and reassuringly about marriage and its many blessings and said he felt that God's graces were more than apparent in both of us and that our marriage should be very successful so long as we did it

His way. Also last night I went to see Mrs White. Did you know she has just had a baby? It is quite the prettiest I have ever seen for a week-old. She, too, noticed the ring and said how pleased she was for us.

It was good to hear you have been doing some research on what houses are available in Frome but I was rather concerned at how difficult it is proving to find a happy medium. It is all very well for the Estate Agent to show you around very nice houses which are seventy pounds per year to rent. That is 27 shillings a week, and you only earn 25 shillings, don't forget! Then at the other end of the scale – small, economic properties for six shillings and sixpence are all very well, but not, I think, if they do not have a bathroom! Still, I do understand that all this searching for houses takes up lots of time and is very wearing and I KNOW you will find somewhere just perfect for the two of us before long. When that is done, we can let our parents know what we have in mind regarding getting on with the wedding sooner, in September, rather than later with all the associated waiting and waiting when there is no point in that, is there? Perhaps it would be a good idea to invite them down to spend a week or so in the West Country in July, maybe staying a night or two with your people while they are here?

Well I am afraid I must go now as I have a lesson at 5.15p.m. and it is already 5.20p.m.!

All My Love and ten thousand kisses,
Noreen.

Cecil stares at the thin curtains into which streaks of light, the beginning of the dawn, are throwing pale, eerie patterns. Dawn does not come early in February. He must have been drowsing and breakfast may not be far off. But there is time. There will be time before breakfast to read at least one more letter. The letter is another written in warmer time, the month of June.

129

My Darling,

I could not wait to get away from Sister Immaculata after tea, she was chattering on about – well, I don't know what (she's lovely really, of course) – but all the time I was just aching to get to you again, even in this very unsatisfactory way.

It is so marvellous just after you have left me because your presence is still with me – in my mind I can hear you still saying such lots of things, nice things like, "Oh, my sweetest, most beautiful Noreen," and "Will we be happy do you think?" and I can see your eyes looking at me as if you loved me, oh, so much, so very, very much and I can feel your hands and your arms and your lips and your body until I nearly cry out for you again and all the time you are going further away from me, back to Frome, and Mrs Bird at your lodgings, and Mr Brown at your office the next day, and all the same old drab, loveless existence.

Sometimes, when you feel fed-up, stop for a moment, relax mentally and feel me loving and loving and loving you, as I am doing all the time, and then perhaps you will feel better. You know you are the only being in the world that MATTERS to me. I mean lots of people make up my life, and I am quite fond of lots of them – but nobody is indispensable to me, as you are. You are the one person I really feel I could not do without.

Always, when you leave me to go on to Frome and I go into Benediction, I get a terrible, sudden fear that you might be killed on the way and I begin praying frantically that you will arrive safely. Sometimes I feel quite alarmed when I realise how much we do mean to each other – we have a little world of our very, very own, haven't we? No-one will ever know just exactly all that there is between us, no-one could ever understand you or me just exactly as we understand each other. We are building up something of our own which will always last, which no-one can ever take from us. We must go on building up nicer and nicer secrets of our own so that when we are old, God willing, we will have something between us which no-one else can ever touch or share in. I don't mean that we must get selfishly wrapped up in each other, we will I hope have lots of other people in our lives and enjoy things with them, but it will be nice to have a "retiring chamber" of memories of our own where we will be able to leave the rest of the world outside.

It is only 5.30p.m. – I have had a sudden idea. I shall post this tonight, now, so that you will get it tomorrow morning. Will that be a nice surprise for you, my darling?

I have just been trying to imagine your face and expression as you read this and I see your half-sad expression, the one that makes me feel as though my heart will break. Probably you disagree, but I often think I am very weak-willed where you are concerned. I mean I deny you something and then that expression comes and makes me want to lay myself beneath your feet and beg of you to do just what you like with me.

Do you know I almost long for tomorrow that I might return a little to normal because, feeling as I do at the moment, I just can't exist without you. I want to beg of you to come back next week-end to marry me even if we do have nowhere to live as yet, to stay with me forever and ever. But tomorrow these tumultuous thoughts will be once again under control. I will work and laugh and talk as though no such thought has ever crossed my mind – perhaps it would have been wise to have left this letter until tomorrow – because tonight I love you so utterly and unbearably.

Goodbye, my very own, I love you with all my heart,
Noreen.

"And I love you," Cecil mumbles into his pillow. "See you in the morning." Cecil carefully folds the letter along the original crease-lines. Replaces it in the envelope. On the outside of the envelope there is an inscription. 'S.A.G.' The same inscription to be found on every letter which Noreen sent him. 'Saint Anthony Guide'. Let Saint Anthony Guide the letter safely to its destination. And Saint Anthony did; so far as Cecil knows, guided every letter to him. None were lost. A tribute to the efficiency of the Post Office too, he thinks. Yes, quite a record.

"HOW ARE YOU TODAY, DARLING?"

Noreen bustles into Cecil's room and speaks without giving herself time to divest herself of her latest purchases, an overcoat with a tartan design and a mohair scarf. She has arrived earlier than usual. Stepping quickly to the side of his bed, she takes Cecil's head gently between her hands.

"Hoi! What are you doing?"

"I've been worried about you, C."

Cecil cannot hear Noreen's reply because she still has her hands over his ears.

"I can't hear you."

Noreen removes her hands reluctantly.

"You slept right through yesterday. We couldn't wake you, whatever we did."

Cecil tries to remember what he did yesterday, without success.

"And it was so unusual for you – you usually like Saturdays because they're quieter, don't you?"

"Ye'm..."

"We nearly called the Doctor."

"Good gracious me. Thank goodness you didn't. No need... No need at all..."

"I'm so relieved. I really am."

Noreen takes off her coat and scarf and drapes them over the end of Cecil's bed, but leaves on her tartan beret with its long, curving pheasant feather. She looks through the window towards Penarth Head. Cecil notices that her shoulders, which have been anxiously hunched up, are gradually lowering.

"It's nice and clear by the headland today," she says finally, enjoying the return to normality; to the reassuring familiarity of comments and phrases which she uses and repeats, with minor adjustments and variations, on most days.

"Ye'm... Is it?"

Cecil's facial expression suggests he is still getting over the shock of Noreen's entrance and what appeared to him to be her excessive concern over him catching up on some sleep. Then, he realises, if he slept through Saturday, today must be Sunday.

"Have we been down to Mass yet?"

"Not yet, darling. We'll be going down shortly. Incidentally, that reminds me of what I was going to tell you yesterday, before you did your Rip Van Winkle act."

"Some news 'm?"

"Well, not news, exactly. I've enquired about lunch at The Copthorne, for our anniversary later this month. You know the newish hotel at Culverhouse Cross."

"'ve never been there..."

"It's a nice modern place. And they haven't got lots of steps or anything awkward like that. I rang and checked."

"Ah... 'm."

"Well... are you pleased?"

"Ummm... I'm just thinking about... I don't think I could go without..."

"There's a taxi firm, Black Cabs, which can take you in your chair."

"Ah..."

"Oh, do say you'll come, C. Everything'll be fine!"

"Well, I'd like to take you out for our anniversary. How many is it, now?"

"59."

"No! Really? 59... Well, well..."

"That's it then. It's decided. We'll book it for the

Monday, not the Saturday, it'll be quieter and Sean will be at work of course, so it'll just be the two of us..."

"Oh... y'em."

After Mass, Noreen explains to Cecil she has arranged to have lunch at the home of one of her friends in Llandaff and wants to pop home first to get ready. Cecil has a little time before lunch. He reaches for his box of letters. Even now, all these years later, a wave of emotion goes through him as he looks at the handwriting on the next letter. His name and address has been recorded in an angular hand-writing, sloping sharply forward and in thick, black ink. It is a letter from Noreen's father, Jack Byrne. Awe is too strong a word to describe how he felt when he received this letter. Confusion is better, he thinks.

Bristol.
Friday, 7th July 1939.

Dear Cecil

I expect you will be surprised to get this letter from me.

I know that you realise that your engagement to Noreen, while perhaps at the time giving us a shock, as I told you gives us pleasure and you have our approval, but now I come to the cause of this letter – the date of your marriage.

Noreen's mother and I, when we had time to think things over, decided that September was far too soon and that you should wait until next year. Noreen is all we have and we can't think of her being taken from us so quickly. In fact we have not slept since, thinking of it.

Perhaps you may accuse me of changing my mind from what I said at Minehead during our day out over there with you and Noreen last Wednesday, and from what we agreed when at your parents' home the day before, but any approval I gave there was given under a kind of pressure and with a poor heart. We were at Chard last night and I may say upset

Noreen very much, but she is now agreeable to wait until next year. Which I think is best for all and will give you and Noreen nice time to get your home together, which is a greater responsibility than you think.

I expect you will be seeing Noreen tomorrow so don't reply to this until you have had a chat with her.

We are, as you can see from the address at the top of this letter, on our way back to Rhosllanerchrugog. We have enjoyed our holiday very well, but not this last few days.

Yours sincerely,

J. Byrne.

Cecil remembers driving down from Frome to Chard immediately, to see how Noreen was feeling about things. As her father had put in his letter, she was very much upset. However, when all was said and done, she had little option but to accept her father's suggestion that they should delay their wedding plans. Cecil himself was very busy at the time, he recalls, organising a trip to Cleeve Abbey with the Civil Service Catholic Guild which was to take place the next day. After Noreen had vented her frustration, they had decided the best thing would be for Noreen to write a letter to her father the next day acknowledging the wisdom of his advice and thus putting his mind at rest as soon as possible, along with a short note to Cecil's parents, just to bring them up to date. They had both felt desperately disappointed. As if the strength of their love had somehow been called into question. But they had tried to understand how it must feel for Noreen's parents, not having had a lot of warning, and that her father would have to be weighing up the financial implications of the reception and so on. Cecil felt Noreen had coped extraordinarily well with the situation, taking into account all the circumstances.

My Dearest Cecil,

I have just finished the difficult task of writing to Daddy – and I don't really see how he could say no to my new suggestion, I have put it so nicely – let's hope he won't say no anyway. I started with the usual pleasantries of course with which I won't bore you, then I have written rather vaguely, "...what about making the wedding some time around Christmas, Daddy?", so we'll see what he has to say about that.

What a nice day you have had for your tour to Cleeve Abbey. When I had finished writing Daddy's letter and looked out, I almost regretted not having come with you. By the way, isn't it rather unusual to have it on a Sunday? Or is it styled 'a pilgrimage'?

MONDAY.

I desisted yesterday for want of something to say – nothing had happened and my thoughts were such conflicting and provoking ones that they could not be written down. Today it is not much better so how I am going to fill the two remaining pages I cannot imagine.

I have just been to get my cards changed, renewed, or whatever is the current term. The girl at the Labour Exchange looked at me in surprise and cheerily said, "Hello, you're still here then..." To her surprise, I bitterly replied, "Yes, and likely to be here for quite a lot longer..."

I have not written to your parents yet. I thought perhaps it would be more appropriate were you to do so, when you have a bit more time. In fact, I am afraid I shall not be able to write to you again this week, as we have started exams and I am already up to my neck in corrections. I had forgotten all about them as I did not have to prepare the papers this term;

we are using the same ones as the exam people are having.

I suppose you and I are still going on Saturday for our weekend in Lostwithiel? – anyhow write and give me full directions in your own detailed and inimitable way.

Goodbye, my sweet – à Samedi.

Lots of Love

Noreen.

P.S. Let me know if you hear from Daddy.

His ability to immerse himself in his work set him in good stead at that difficult time, Cecil thinks. It was a very long week. Not knowing how Noreen's father would respond to her letter. Eventually, Noreen had written to him again, the following Friday. It was the only time he had delayed opening one of her letters. His anxiety was that Noreen's father would be so incensed by her counter-suggestion that the wedding should be at Christmas, instead of the following year, that he might withdraw his consent to their marriage altogether. He was also worried that her father would blame Cecil for what Noreen had suggested in her letter, when in fact it had only loosely approximated to what he had expected her to write. He had finally plucked up courage and, holding his breath, opened the letter very slowly.

'The Senior Classroom'
St Gildas' Convent,
Chard.
Friday July 14th, 1939.

My Own,

I suppose when you see this envelope you will know that it contains the "fatal news"!!! I heard from Daddy this morning and the news is middlin' good. Perhaps it is best if

I let you decide for yourself... I quote verbatim:

'...Mother and I were glad to see by your letter that you have agreed to wait a while and to reverse your idea of getting married in September. About the third week in February would be a suitable date in the New Year, we felt. You could come home for the Christmas and that will give you the proper time in residence in Rhosllanerchrugog... How about my giving you away to Cecil on the 27th February?... I wrote to Cecil on the Saturday from Bristol. It was an effort, I assure you, writing in the bustle of the G.P.O. and quite a few of the staff eyeing me up, thinking I was planting a bomb for the I.R.A. to blow up the G.P.O., but I wanted to write to Cecil as I did NOT WANT ANY MISUNDERSTANDINGS (Daddy's capital letters, not mine) that we were against the marriage.'

And that is more or less all there was, apart from a few generalities not concerned with the main issue.

What do you think of it? Will you resign yourself? Or is it still asking too much?

Just had a long interruption concerning which questions had to be done and which allowed a choice, and it has disturbed my train of thought, so I think I will say goodbye – Oh Lord, and just then Mother Superior came in and found me sinning against the 11th Commandment – 'Thou shalt not write letters to your betrothed when thou shouldst be teaching your class' – it used to be very strictly against my principles to do anything like this, at one time.

Darling, I am going to make a cake for the competition at 4.30p.m. – if it survives, I'll give you a bit and you'll want to marry me next week – you do NOW though, don't you? I really MUST GO.

I love you,
Noreen.

They did not go to Lostwithiel together that weekend or the following weekend, Cecil is certain about that. He and

Noreen decided they needed to spend some time with her parents to calm things down again. They had travelled up together and stayed at Norland in Rhosllanerchrugog. Time had passed gently doing ordinary things together: they had played partner whist – her parents were great whist players; Noreen had played the piano for them – Beethoven, Bach, and some Irish melodies; they had listened to the radio – Jack Byrne was very fond of tuning-in to Athlone. Then, over a cup of tea before going to bed, they had settled on the 27th February as the wedding date, in line with Jack Byrne's wishes, as if it were the most obvious choice in the world.

Although Cecil was happy that a final decision had been made, he was sorry that they were going to have to wait nearly seven more months before marrying. In April, all men of twenty and 21 had been called up. It had felt unreal – on the one hand to be living a life normally, as if nothing untoward were happening; on the other, to be reading, each day, of the threat of war moving ever closer. He missed Noreen in the week so much. They were very much in love. During the long summer holidays, Noreen was at home with her parents or elsewhere. There seemed so little point in waiting. However, as always, he found great solace in keeping busy and often took office-work with him to his digs in Frome and thus became highly regarded by his superior, Mr Brown.

Though the delay in their marriage plans caused them great pain, Cecil recalls that the delay only served to heighten their anticipation of how wonderful their marriage and married life would be, and gave them more time to enjoy looking forward to the happiness they were convinced it would bring into both their lives. Noreen was never downhearted for long and Cecil turns to her next letter to raise his own spirits.

My Dearest Cecil,

It's 9.45p.m. – I have just been tossing up whether to go to bed or to write to you – and strange to say you won, though I am afraid I feel very Sunday afternoonish after a large, late dinner and with a slumbering form not far away on the settee (Daddy). It has just occurred to me that last Sunday afternoon you were here, what did we do?(!!), can't remember – it must have been a very sedate day, seems simply ages ago!

Thank you for your nice long letter during the week. Mother brought it up to me before I was awake, mostly because she wanted to know if my cousin from Dublin, Cronin, had called on you in Frome as he said he might. What a nice time you gave him and his friend. Cronin wrote during the week and was very thrilled about the visit. Thank you so much, darling, for looking after my relations so well. What a brainwave taking them to Downside Abbey, did you know he is interested in entering the priesthood? And what tremendous luck being able to see the whole of Downside. I felt horribly envious and look forward to seeing Cronin to bombard him with questions. He has written twice now actually and still seems to be enjoying his perambulations around the country.

I was wishing so terribly much that you had been with me in Liverpool during the week, it was great fun and the shops were SO interesting, particularly the furniture shops. There were lots of windows completely furnished as dining rooms, lounges, etc., a great many in that light wood and they really looked rather scrumptious, and lashings of curtains, carpets, eiderdowns, bedspreads etc. that positively made my mouth water, but usually the prices were pretty fantastic. I got most of the things I wanted, with the exception of house coats, even the material for my wedding dress. Mother says it is an extremely bad sign, my getting ready so far in advance, she is afraid something is going to go wrong, but then, of course, there are sure to be dozens of things that I shall leave until the last minute, aren't there?

On Thursday evening we went to New Brighton to see Sister de Chantal, my old Headmistress in the Convent in Wrexham and one of the big influences in my life. Actually I wanted to break the news to her but unfortunately she had gone away to stay at Pantasaph Convent. I saw another Sister at New Brighton and she suggested I went to Pantasaph to see de Chantal, so I am going sometime next week. There is one thing and that is – you really will have to be inspected by her before I marry you because all the big steps in my life so far have been taken with her cognisance and approval. But how could ANYONE do ANYTHING but approve of you.

Nota. Mother has never stopped telling me how handsome you looked in your new suit. I wonder if you would have chosen navy without any outside influence?

Yesterday I had an old schoolfriend, Kathleen, and her husband to tea – Do you remember the one we spoke of at Easter? She was married while you were here. We did enjoy ourselves because they were telling me all the trials and tribulations of married life. Kathleen's story of her first dinner was lovely – it was a complete fiasco! The meat burned to a cinder, the carrots were thick with salt, and the pudding was not done. It seems only the potatoes were edible. They were very amused about it but Arthur, the husband, very sweetly said that that was the only wreck, all the rest had been marvellous. So you will say nice things like that about me, won't you? They are living somewhere near London and pay twenty seven shillings a week for a flat – two rooms and a kitchenette – and they think they are getting it awfully cheap.

Of course, Daddy had to drag me into Wrexham yesterday and my progress through the centre of town was like a triumphal march. Everyone I know seemed to be in town and to have heard I was engaged, so I was stopped and congratulated goodness knows how often. Two more invitations out to tea resulted – I don't mind going out, the trouble is the invitations have to be returned and it eats into one's time so!

Clare Kolb has Laurie staying over with her and she has asked me to go around this evening. I am rather curious to see Laurie as mother has raved about how he has improved since he came back from France. I am looking forward to finding out in what way he has improved! I can't imagine!

By the way, Uncle Hugh got so fed up with 'Watchet' that he came home early, on the Wednesday, vowing never to go there again. He said there was absolutely NOTHING at all there worth watching!

Any more thoughts about you and me going on hols together? Daddy was suggesting at dinner that I went to Ireland for a week. I said I couldn't afford it and he said he'd treat me so I do not know whether I shall be able to resist such a tempting offer. I'll see how the spirit moves me when I see my cousin Cronin and make enquiries as to what his sister, Maire, is doing. We have all got on like a house on fire on previous occasions when I have visited Ireland. What do you say, sweetness?

I was thinking and wondering about you yesterday. What did you do? Do you know that now when you are not near me only half my mind is on what I do or hear, the other half is sub-consciously with you and yet I know when YOU write you will tell me, "I haven't really had time to miss you," or "Now you are so far away I am quite resigned to doing without you," but I want you urgently – frequently.

Well, I never thought I would write so much. I thought there was positively nothing to tell you. But now I must go, it is time to get a glass of milk before turning in and Mother, I fear, is wide awake and disposed to talk.

Goodbye and God bless you my own.
All my love,
Noreen.

They are late bringing lunch again, Cecil notices. He cannot quite see the hands of his clock, someone must have moved it to the windowsill when he wasn't looking, but the determined way his stomach keeps rumbling is a sure sign that it is time to eat.

For the first time he admits to himself that he had not really realised just how many letters Noreen sent him. He is touched by their sheer quantity. But never before has it taken so much time to leaf through them. It usually only takes him a few minutes each day. He resolves to complete the task as usual, before their anniversary, however laboriously he has to toil to do so. Sometimes he wonders what he put in his letters to annoy Noreen, and it gives him pause for thought. Yet there was never anything that made him want to criticise Noreen, of that he is sure. And he will read the letters. Every one. A labour of love, this year above all others.

Norland,
15, Clive Road,
Rhosllanerchrugog.
August 8th, 1939.

My Dearest Cecil,

Such a long time since I have written properly, isn't it? But then I have been so very occupied this week and I have had very solid reasons for being so too, and you will have to excuse me because you yourself must admit it is difficult to find time to write in any but a breathless and hurried manner – as witness your last two letters, and then, as far as I can perceive, you have had nothing to upset the even tenor of your ways until Saturday anyhow, so what can be expected of me with visitors to look after and entertain (Note: no bitterness or rancour intended, only a certain mild reproof)?

Now, let me see, I really ought to have lots to tell you but do not know where to begin. I wrote a week last Sunday, n'est-ce-pas? Well, on Monday the only thing I did was to pay a visit to the Wrexham Convent. Luckily, Sister de Chantal was there and I relieved her and the other good nuns of their anxiety as to whether I had made a suitable match. Sister Angelica was very pleased with me because I had chosen a Catholic but I enlightened her as to your other virtues as well, so she was pleased about them too. I won't tell you what the virtues were!

On Monday night I went down to my Aunt Sarah's. You remember my cousin Frank is marrying a French girl, Simone. Well I met Monsieur and Madame, Simone's parents, at Aunt Sarah's. We had a lovely evening, they are the sweetest people and incidentally they left a very pressing invitation for you and me to go and see them if ever we are in Paris.

On Tuesday I saw a daft film called 'Sweethearts'. The only interesting thing about it being that it was in Technicolour, the first I have seen.

On Wednesday evening we had a very interesting visitor – a Father Cooke from Dublin who was giving a retreat to the nuns. He was a real character – I haven't enjoyed anyone so much for ages. I will tell you lots of funny things about him when I see you (WHEN I see you).

My cousin Cronin and his pal, Andy, arrived on Thursday and since then my hands have been full. We had great fun. Went to the flicks on Friday and, when we got back, Father Cooke was here again. He is based not far from Maynooth, just outside Dublin, and there was such talking, with Daddy there too of course, and exclamations of "Do you know so-and-so..." etc., Andy had to be back for Sunday so went on Saturday morning but Cronin went only this morning.

We had Father Cooke again on Sunday night and yesterday we all went to Chester to the Sports. It was a lovely day and we met Uncle Hugh and my cousin from Cheltenham.

In between all this I have been able to see Clare and Laurie a couple of times (Laurie is so mature now, with a voice like brown chocolate!), and I have cooked, made beds and washed up ad infinitum, so haven't I been busy?

Incidentally – about cooking! I made a cake on Thursday afternoon. The boys came that evening and mother decided to give them some for tea. To my great chagrin, they polished off every crumb at one sitting, and between bites Andy would gulp "Cecil is a very lucky man... a very lucky man... oh, yes, sure he is."

By the way, Cronin was talking about getting the Papal Blessing for our wedding – he was not quite sure about the procedure so we asked Father Cooke on Sunday night and he said he would get it for us. It would be nice wouldn't it? You get a very nice Certificate with a picture of the Pope, etc. on it. It makes a nice souvenir.

Your aunts in Lytham-St-Anne's wrote to me this morning about going to stay with them. I am afraid it is not going to be possible, much though I would have loved to do so, because Cronin has asked me to stay a week in Ireland. He wanted me to go back with him, but I hadn't time to get ready, so I am going a week today, on the 15th August, probably, or it may be the week after. You won't mind will you? He has promised to take me to Galway and to visit my country relations on the farm in Baltinglass, Co. Wicklow, if I go, so I could not resist.

How about our hols? What is going to happen? And when are you coming to see me? I am sick of not seeing you. I suppose it would be quite impossible for you to come and see me this weekend? I ask because the following week-end I might be in Ireland and there's only one more before your holidays start after that.

Anyhow, write to me soon or I'll bust.

Goodbye my only one, a million kisses and every little bit of my love.

God bless you,

Noreen.

'A million kisses'. Cecil had to survive on those kisses while Noreen went to Ireland, he remembers sadly. Although he kept busy to take his mind off things, there were nights when he did not sleep well during those weeks, when he had nightmares, nightmares about losing Noreen, nightmares which he shared with nobody.

He had repeated fears that Noreen might meet someone new. Someone with a soft Irish tongue, a persuasive personality with a thriving business and a sailing cruiser in Dublin Bay on which he liked to entertain his many lady friends, whom Noreen would fall head-over-heels in love with, suddenly recognising how stultifying were Cecil's awkwardness, rigidity and lack of imagination. If she did not meet someone new, Cecil's other horror was that she would get closer and closer to Cronin's friend, Andy. Andy was not planning to be a priest, even if Cronin was. They had such fun when they were all together, the three of them. More spontaneously, he sensed, than when he and Noreen had fun. She went across to Ireland, this date is carved deeply in his memory, on Monday, 14th August 1939.

It had been left to her father to let him know that she had gone because Noreen had apparently been in such a tizzy getting to her train in time, she had only remembered to ask Jack Byrne to drop Cecil a line at the very last minute.

When he rang Noreen's cousin's house in Dublin on Friday, 18th August, 1939, at 11.15p.m. to speak to Noreen, Cecil was told she was still out. That was 'my darkest hour', before the war started, Cecil reminisces.

He had been like a robot at his lodgings in Frome the following morning. His landlady, Mrs Bird, had asked him, "Are you alright, Mr Connolly? Would you like some camomile, dear?" He had replied, "No, no. I'm quite alright, thank you, Mrs Bird, and I don't need any camomile." Unusually brusque, Cecil thinks. Mrs Bird was such a devoted soul, a widow; always so kind and attentive to her 'guests' as she called them. That same day, at 12.35pm, a telegram had been delivered to Mrs Bird's door, addressed to Connolly, 54, Somerset Road, Frome. It read, "DARLING – A THOUSAND APOLOGIES AND A MILLION THANKS. LOVE NOREEN." It had been sent at 11.05a.m. from Foxrock Post Office, Dublin.

The telegram only exacerbated Cecil's worry about what was going on. It was clear that something had gone wrong, without any explanation of what the problem was. Cecil had driven home to Chard later, to spend the night with his parents. His mother had immediately seen some-thing was wrong, simply from the expression in his eyes. "Twas! What is it?" she had said immediately. "Nothing, nothing at all," he had replied and so his mother had said to his father it was best to leave him to himself, to be quiet. Cecil had gone into the garden shed and worked with his fretwork tools for several hours, something he had not done for some years. He made a beautiful toast rack which he gave to his parents. After that he felt a bit better, at least able to converse normally with Mammy Connolly.

Cecil had then received a full letter from Noreen on Monday 21st August, 1939, which had been written on the Saturday.

2, Brighton Road,
Foxrock,
Dublin.
Saturday 19th August, 1939.

My Dearest Cecil,

Wasn't it a positive tragedy about my being out last night when you phoned? Actually we did not get back until nearly twelve and the minute Bridie (she's the maid) saw me she said a gentleman had called me from Somerset. I nearly wept with disappointment when I realised it must have been you!

I know what a long time it usually takes to get through. Darling I AM sorry, so very, very sorry. But I must tell you that Bridie is a very nice girl and a marvellous cook, so you did get something for your money!

Thank you a million times though, it was a great thrill to know you had phoned me even though I did not actually speak to you.

Incidentally – they very much want me to stay until Sunday week, the 27th August. Life is very good here. It may be in extremely bad taste to mention it but Cronin and Maire's parents are undoubtedly what Daddy would call 'very comfortably off'. Their parents, Uncle Jim and Auntie Dolores, own several Off Licenses which are said to be flourishing. As you may imagine, it is taking me some time to become used to the ministrations of Bridie, after being used to cleaning and washing-up all the time at home, but I can easily imagine myself adapting very well to having afternoon tea served in the drawing room each day, given sufficient time here!

We are going to Galway for a few days tomorrow, I think, and it would mean my rushing straight back and home, if I left on Wednesday. I don't know what to do, because I am hoping you will come up to Rhosllanerchrugog next weekend; if you are able to do so, I shall come home, if you cannot do so I might stay here until Sunday week. See? So could you write by return to Foxrock then it could be forwarded to Galway and I would get it by Wednesday and could come home the same day or on Thursday anyway. The thing I should like best would be to see you.

By the way, would you also please re-explain in your letter

all that business about holidays because Bridie was rather vague about what the message was exactly and I am not too clear about it, but I do know my very own sweet that it will be very, very difficult to get away sooner than we arranged.

Now, I suppose, I might start telling you something of what I've been doing since I came. Well, on Wednesday night we went for a drive to see some typical Irish scenery. That was fine. I love the countryside, as you know. However, I must admit it simply served to confirm my opinion that one Irish field looks remarkably like any other, or like any West Country field, or for that matter any Welsh field, especially as darkness falls!

On Thursday, I had a positively marvellous time. We went to a place called Brittas Bay near Wicklow Town. It was a perfect day and a perfect place – something like Cornwall, ever so many little coves, rocks and marvellous sand, but it was better than Cornwall because the sea was not so tumultuous so that we could bathe in comfort. After bathing, we found a little spot in the sandhills, shaped like a basin with very steep sides. Cronin had a Lilo and he and Andy took turns in pulling Maire and me down the sides, sitting on the Lilo, at about 30 m.p.h. It WAS fun, I haven't enjoyed myself so much for ages. I got very sunburnt too, but this time I took precautions and creamed myself well before sunbathing.

Yesterday we went to visit some of my relations in the country, the farm is enormous and runs alongside a beautiful river. My Uncle Mick was keen to show me around as he always is and, by the time we got back to the farmhouse, I was absolutely exhausted from just walking around the farm. Later, we called at Mount Street for supper and found a friend of Cronin's there, not Andy, a chap called Finbarr studying Classics at Trinity College, so we stayed talking with him and how he could talk, and then we had to take him home and that is what kept us late.

And today I am writing to you – but I must stop and write to Mummy and Daddy too. If I had their address I'd send a card to your people – but I haven't, so give them my love and tell your father I saw Lugnaquilla Mountain yesterday. He always brings it up when Ireland is mentioned. I think he just likes saying the words really, all those liquid vowels.

Goodbye, my darling. I think of you constantly, you are not to think for one minute that I am forgetting you or loving you less – on the contrary – goodbye and God bless you, my own. And write to me by return – don't forget!

All My Love,
Noreen.

Noreen remained in Ireland for about two weeks in all. Eventually, she came back to the mainland. Cecil's pleasure at hearing from the nuns that Noreen was back in Rhosllanerchrugog at the end of August was soon overshadowed by the consternation he and everyone else in Britain felt upon Germany invading Poland. The authorities had already issued gas masks, had trenches dug, sandbagged important buildings and built public air raid shelters. But everybody was hoping against hope that they would never be needed. Then, it had been inevitable, on Sunday, the 3rd September, 1939, Britain and France had declared war on Germany.

September 1939

NOREEN had written to Cecil on the day war broke out. Cecil notices that the post mark on the envelope shows the time of 7.55pm on that momentous day, so the letter had been posted before then. The war only hours old and Noreen's first thought had been for him. His reaction, he recalls, was very mixed. Glad that he would be seeing Noreen soon, but half-wishing she had stayed in the safety of Ireland.

Norland,
15, Clive Road,
Rhosllanerchrugog.
Sunday, 3rd September, 1939.

My Dearest Love,
Well, there is no more hope left, except to hope that it will not last long.

I am returning to Chard next Saturday. Perhaps I will be able to see you at Bristol, or, failing that, can you drive down to Chard next weekend?

This can only be a very short note as we already have one of our evacuated children with two more to follow, and Mother is out all the time getting them to billets so that we are kept terribly busy.

I am hoping to hear from you tomorrow. I have so much to say but writing seems terribly inadequate and there is so little time. A lot of the children look so lost and pathetic with their parcels of belongings, it is ever so sad, especially seeing the smaller ones who are often unable to stop themselves from shedding a quiet tear. Say a prayer for them.

God Bless You and Keep You Safe through all this,
All My Love,
Noreen.

The following Saturday, Cecil had driven from Frome to Bristol, to collect Noreen and drive her down to the convent in Chard. He remembers clutching her in his arms as he had never done before, standing on the platform at Bristol Station, with other people streaming around them, faces suddenly drawn and serious, and wisps of steam curling around them threateningly, like seepage from a dormant volcano.

They had each ordered a cup of coffee and a pork pie in a cafe on Blackboy Hill near the Downs, before driving out of Bristol, and it was there, in the cafe, that they had shared their reactions to the news of the war, and discovered that they felt exactly the same – insofar as it affected them. Cecil feels a surge of joy, even now, at the memory of the sense of utter unity which they had experienced. He had been feeling so alone, he recalls, at the prospect that the war would mean separation from Noreen one way or another.

In their haste to say it, they nearly talked over each other.

"We must get married, now... mustn't we darling?" Noreen was looking earnestly into Cecil's eyes.

"I think we should... I really think we should. We have no way of knowing what this war will mean... Even if we married tomorrow our happiness could be terribly short-lived."

As they drove to Chard, they had talked about the awfulness of the war, the unnecessary deaths it would cause, how countless thousands of innocent people would be caught up in it against their will, how maybe even millions would die before it would be over, as had been the case in the First World War (yes, it did turn out to be millions who died, Cecil reflects). They had felt sadness and anger that a war should happen at all, should even perhaps be thought necessary. But, having reached swift and total unanimity over what they themselves should do, Cecil was aware of a deep sense of peace within him, something which he hoped would stay with him through thick and thin.

It was only when Cecil had dropped Noreen off in Chard and driven back to Frome that he began to give serious thought to Jack Byrne, and whether for Jack the declaration of war would be sufficient justification to overturn their previous hard-won agreement. What was self-evident to Noreen and Cecil might not be so to Jack Byrne, he had thought, and he had reflected long and hard over the fact that Jack had surprised him once or twice in the past.

When they had been drinking their coffee in Bristol, Noreen had dismissed consideration of what her father might say with a flick of her hand, "He'll just have to understand." Those were her precise words. Cecil is so sure about that because he remembers repeating her words to himself in his lodgings in Frome, trying to summon up the same degree of certainty which Noreen had displayed.

It had not been possible for Cecil to bring his holidays forward to August. They were increasingly short of staff, and Mr Brown was not someone one trifled with when it came to the running of the office. 'Mr Brown-Man-About-Town' had been his nickname, and this had always been varied to 'Mr Brown-Man-About-The-Office' whenever he was being more officious than usual. So Cecil had taken his holiday in Lostwithiel in September, with both his parents. Noreen had been desperately unhappy about it. Her school term had restarted and she had been unable to join him at all.

In some ways Cecil had felt that, although he would

have loved to holiday alone with Noreen, it was perhaps a blessing that it had not been possible, when he considered what Noreen's father might have thought of them holidaying as 'man and wife'.

He had rung the Convent to speak to Noreen, while he was on holiday in Lostwithiel. In her distress, Noreen had said she felt it was as if they had never been engaged – the way they simply continued each living in their parents' pockets. He had understood how she felt. Had felt exactly the same way at the time, he remembers. He had written asking her to try to be patient. She had replied in a way which demonstrated to him the depth of her personality, her ability to look at herself honestly, her humility, her forbearance. I am a lucky man, he thinks to himself. That fellow, Andy, was right. A lucky man, to be sure.

››

Saint Gildas' Convent,
Chard.
Friday 22nd September, 1939.

My Darling Love,

So many, many thanks for your letter – you are right, I think it is being separated that makes us so miserable. I am sending this to Frome so that you receive it on your return from Lostwithiel.

Last night I was thinking that my love for you is so deep and strong, but all these little differences are like tiny grains of sand gradually filling and silting up a deep strong river and leaving it at last only a dull, thin trickle. I could never bear to see that happen and we must make quite sure that it will not, before we allow our two great depths of love to run on together.

Since your letter my heart feels eased, as it were; I am almost happy again – I AM happy in that my confidence in 'us' has returned a hundredfold.

Forgive me for my unkindness when we spoke on the telephone, I know that for you everything you do comes from a wish to do the good and right thing; so for you there is nothing to forgive. Pray fervently that I may learn more patience and resignation. Love me still in spite of my faults. It is so much easier making good resolutions than keeping to them, but I am determined to try, and to keep trying.

God bless and keep you.

Noreen.

P.S. Your heather 'olive branch' is the most precious thing in my possession (apart from my cherished writing case, of course!). Thank you so much.

*

The outbreak of war had made Cecil's separation from Noreen, during his holiday in Lostwithiel, feel so much worse. At the very time when they had recommitted themselves to the idea of marrying as soon as humanly possible, he had taken himself away on holiday with his parents, instead of being at Noreen's side where he had wanted to be. His parents had done hardly anything else during the holiday other than worry about whether Cecil would be drafted into one of the armed forces and where he might be sent if he were to be.

Mammy had said, "If you do have to go, I just hope it is not into the navy or the air force, out in some boat or up in a plane. I hope it's to the army, so that at least you are able to keep both your feet on dry land." Pop Connolly had snorted when she said this. Cecil had not been sure whether it had been a snort of derision or a stifled sob.

While they were trying to make the best of it in tranquil Lostwithiel, the aircraft carrier HMS Courageous had been sunk by a U-Boat. They had all felt extremely guilty at being on holiday when others were risking and losing their lives. Cecil recalls feeling as if he was in some way a malingerer. He was a young man in good health and could as easily have been serving his country as these others. For Pop Connolly it brought back his guilt over surviving the first war, when men whom he had known well had died. Cecil had assumed this about his father, rather than hearing it from Pop himself, and he remembers finding it hard to understand that the news about HMS Courageous had not prompted a greater reaction. He would have expected Pop to say more. "Those poor lads..." is all Pop actually said, but he had sat very still for a long time, in the bay window of the pine cabin they had rented for the week.

Cecil had only been back at work in Frome for seven days when Jack Byrne shattered his peace of mind regarding the wedding plans. So far as Noreen and Cecil were concerned, their wedding was now to take place in the third or fourth week of October. Cecil knew Noreen had written to her father telling him this and giving the reasons why they had decided to bring the date forward and, not having heard anything to the contrary, Cecil had begun to assume that they had Jack Byrne's blessing. Jack's letter had arrived at Cecil's lodgings in Frome on the Saturday morning.

Cecil notices that Jack Byrne's writing is even more jagged than usual, and that there are some words missed out, as if the letter had been written in a hurry, or even in a fit of temper, and had not been read over.

Norland,
15, Clive Road,
Rhosllanerchrugog
Thursday, 28th September, 1939.

Dear Cecil,

We received Noreen's letter and rather surprised to see by same that you and Noreen still thinking of your marriage this year, so taking Noreen to live with you in Frome.

I may say at once, I don't agree. Before we thought of a war I only gave my consent very reluctantly, but now we have a war on I am all the more against it, be the war long or short.

If the war is going to be long, it is a thousand to one you will have to go. It would be a pretty mess if, six months after you were married, you had to join up and leave Noreen miles from us, here in Rhosllanerchrugog, and miles from your parents, down there in Chard. If either set of parents was near, there might be an excuse.

And if the war is going to be over soon, well you can wait until then. The engagement should in the first place have been given out as twelve months. I see no sacrifice in this.

I don't want to see Noreen's married life a failure, as her teaching has been. She has been wasting her time at Chard, working for next to nothing and no holiday pay. It has been a keen disappointment to us she never used her Teaching Certificate. I am also writing Noreen on this important matter as this rushing business has caused Mrs Byrne and I a lot of worry, but I will say no more on the matter at present... and I hope a little more discussion will be used from now on at the fixing your marriage date.

Yours sincerely,

J. Byrne

Cecil feels the palms of his hands grow sweaty. He reaches for his glass of water. His throat always seems to be dry these days.

He dealt with Jack Byrne's letter as well as he could in the circumstances, he recalls. He had rued his inability to talk to his own father about such matters but had tried to discuss with Mammy what he should say or do. She had said, "Well, well... we're funny mortals, aren't we, Twas? It'll be alright... you'll see. So long as Noreen and you love each other... it will all work out, I'm sure."

In the end, he had decided to write back to Jack Byrne to the effect that he would discuss his letter with Noreen in due course, as if he were writing a business letter at the office.

Again, he and Noreen had little choice but to accept that they would have to wait, hoping that the war would be over quickly. Cecil saw it all as a test of their love – a test he was determined to pass.

Noreen had soon subdued her fury over what she felt was her father's bovine attitude to their marriage plans, but somehow the idea of an October wedding died. The joy of planning it had been crushed by Jack Byrne's response, and to go against Noreen's parents' wishes was unthinkable.

Cecil was surprised how, once the immediate panic about the war was over, life for both of them had returned almost to normal, apart from the obvious things like petrol rationing and the black-out.

He picks up Noreen's next letter and it reminds him just how strongly ordinary life, work, conversations with friends, and simple social events, still dominated their waking hours, despite the war; until dramatic reports of battle victories or terrible casualties cut across the weekly rhythm.

There was still the issue of what to do about the wedding. In August, they had known they were getting married the following February. At the end of September, they found themselves in the position of simply having no idea when the date of their marriage was to be. Cecil knew how he felt towards Noreen whether he was called up or not, and wherever he might have to serve in the world. And, to her credit, Noreen never gave up trying to sort their wedding date out, Cecil recalls.

Saint Gildas' Convent,
Chard.
Sunday, 8th October, 1939.

Darling,

I feel so mean and unkind not having written to you yesterday, but I was just going to write to you on Friday night when the girls asked me to go down for a while to look at the play they are doing for Mother Superior's Feast Day, and it kept me until suppertime when it was too late to write. I almost 'phoned you yesterday but decided not to. It is not much fun 'phoning you from Chard because I have to be so careful what I say. But really I am sorry about not writing.

Thank you for your letter, which was, to say the least of it, slightly incoherent, but I enjoy them like that. Do you know, I was just thinking you rarely give people their names? You always say, "the chap from Plymouth", not "Williams, the chap from Plymouth", or "the married fellow with the baby, who lives in those new houses I showed you", not "Mr Duncan, the married fellow... etc." It is a bit eccentric of you, "...youthful man, currently residing in Frome with an Austin Seven car..." But as you are not so impersonal in your dealings with me, I shall forgive you with alacrity.

I expect you want to know my activities of the week, but the only thing of interest is the First Aid lecture on Friday night – three of the sisters came, much to my disappointment! My friend of the curly hair and the sweet smile was there (I don't know his name yet). I sat behind the Sisters and made eyes at him all night (!). Willy sat next to me, he's that young man with freckles and tousled locks who always sits with his parents at Mass, two benches from the front. I thought wouldn't it be awful if people thought I was engaged to him!

The First Aid lecture itself was very interesting and now, darling, if you break your leg I should know how to treat you AND I know two pressure points where bleeding can be stopped.

On the way home, Mr Woods and another teacher from Chard tacked themselves on to me even though we were only about five yards from the Sisters all the way, I expect they think I am very abandoned. You need not bother about getting jealous, sweetheart, Woods gives me a pain in the neck, he can talk nothing else but 'school' – and himself.

Yesterday was so lovely. Just a touch of Autumn in the air. Sister Maria and I went for a walk around Edencote. It is one of my favourite walks, you get the most beautiful views all the way, and yesterday was so clear and calm we could see more than usual. I was thinking that Chard is a sweet little place, I really think I should like to live here always – under certain circumstances.

I went to the flicks in the evening, with Margaret. We went to see "The Ware Case". You are quite right in saying that a good English film is worth two American ones. It was quite delightful – the plot was interesting, the acting excellent, the accents pleasing to the ear and the photography dignified. You would have enjoyed it – but I have given up recommending films to you, and then, of course, you are working overtime.

I have been feeling rather light-hearted since Friday as I had a letter from Mother – just one of her usual, ordinary, chatty letters with no mention of all the vexatious problems that beset us. I was so relieved to get it as it was a fortnight since she wrote. The only thing she said about the wedding side of things was... "I did not write last week as Daddy wanted to write to you"; SHE did not sound disapproving or anything and, if she was, she did not show it.

11.50a.m. I have just returned from Mass. The Church was absolutely packed. By the way – did you notice a little chap in the Corr's seat, last Sunday? He has been with them a couple of weeks. Well this morning Bridgette button-holed me in the vestibule and told me it was "budding love"! between THEM. I know you have just said, "Who? Who said? How do you know? Who is he? When? Why? What? Where?" But perhaps I under-rate your intelligence. However, I duly admired him and Bridgette gushed all over me for ages – congratulating me, asking about you and so on. I suppose she wouldn't behave like that until she could produce a man too. Monica was there also and, Heaven forgive me, she looked just like a horse. She had on her brown fur coat and her hair was all brushed out, very long and tied in the back of her neck – it did look like a mane. Two such NICE girls, darling, I simply can't imagine how you escaped them. (The above is typical of the cattiness of the female mind – this female mind anyway. I hear you sigh – disgust, your cutting expletives, I am humbled and ashamed).

Do you know, we have forty three boarders! I think it is disgraceful, there is not really enough room for so many – the war again – they will be asking me to give up my room next, let them just dare... It makes such a lot of extra work with corrections; it is a good job petrol is rationed, I think, as I shall probably be working overtime for as long as I'm here and, if you visited as often as we'd like, I'd have no time for anything.

I really ought to write to Daddy soon. What do you want me to say? I mean when are you hoping or expecting to get married, if ever? I must give him some idea and I cannot be firm and unrelenting, unless I know. Oh yes, now you are throwing your eyes heavenwards, falling back in your chair all limp and groaning, "When am I HOPING or EXPECTING to get married?" I know all that, darling, but what I want is for you to tell me precisely what you are thinking, the exact workings of your mind, what, with luck, you expect will happen.

I expect you have not been too lonely this weekend, or have you? To me it seems like coming to an oasis in the desert and finding no water there and I have to go through all the clogging sand of next week and perhaps even the week after without refreshment. Such a nice simile, don't you think?

The worst of it is you feel so remote, I can't even think what you look like, the only thing I can see is the funny way your hair parted last week. In fact, my own, I think I am becoming completely impersonal, or perhaps it is just your feelings of being impersonal which have communicated themselves to me. Last week-end (was it only last week-end?) seems like something which happened a hundred years ago. You know, I think I am fed-up.

Anyhow, there's the bell, so I'm off to feed the inner man.

Write to me nicely soon. I send you all the kisses you would normally have had this week-end – and some more.

All My Love

Noreen.

P.S. I had a letter from your mother yesterday, enquiring about the colour of a bedcover which your aunt wants to give us – I am going to say goldy colour or pale rose as your mother informs me that she has already bought us a green

one – and blankets and sheets and things – did you know?
   N.

His aunt bought them the pale rose bedcover, but it was some time before they received it, Cecil reflects. It was a strange feeling communicating with people about wedding presents, without having a date fixed for the wedding.

Cecil watches Noreen's back as she leaves his room. He calls to her.

"Will I see you later?"

Noreen does not hear him. He hears her voice talking to some of the staff down the corridor. Perhaps she has only gone to get him some fresh water for the flower vases. The pot plant has really come on, he notices. Amaryllis belladonna. The bloom seems to have grown half an inch since yesterday and it is a beautiful shade of red. The sound of Noreen's voice fades. She must be going. She may be coming back after lunch, Cecil thinks. Or maybe in the morning. Perhaps he has been drowsing again.

Noreen had written again in November, 1939.

Saint Gildas' Convent,
Chard.
Sunday 12th November, 1939.

My Dearest Love,

There are a thousand things I ought to do before it is time for Mass, but I can do none of them until I write to you.

I have just been reading bits out of 'Romeo and Juliet' – the balcony scene of course, and I thought how nicely Shakespeare says what I wanted to say in my last letter – you remember where Juliet is trying to say goodnight to Romeo – "Goodnight, goodnight! Parting is such sweet sorrow that

167

I shall say goodnight till it be tomorrow." – Terribly like the way I feel sometimes.

Also, I had not read 'Romeo and Juliet' since falling in love, and it makes such a difference!

By the way, talking of poetry, I had some perfectly awful moments the other day. I was reading the girls some poems and wanted to show them how effective repetition could be. There is a thing called "Shule Agrah" which is a good example, and one of the verses goes something like this -

'I laugh to think of him like this,

Who once found all his joy and bliss

Against my heart, against my kiss

Shule, Shule, Shule Agrah!' – When I read that I suddenly found myself beginning to blush and blush and BLUSH. It was awful. I did not dare to look at them for ten minutes. Just look what you've done to me. At one time I should have been no more self-conscious about that than if I had been reading about hens. Henceforward I am going to eschew love poems in class.

Olwen, Margaret and I went to the flicks yesterday to see 'Three Smart Girls Grow Up'! It was good and very funny in places. But you know now, wherever I go and whatever I see, I never really enjoy it fully because you are not there to share it.

I have just discovered a little hole in my stocking. If I do not mend it, it will probably run in to a ladder so I shall leave you for the moment as it is nine o'clock and unless I am ready to take my place in Church by 9.20a.m. – it will have been bagged. Au revoir.

8.45p.m. You would never guess where I have been since I last 'saw' you – to all our favourite haunts: Seaton, Lyme Regis, down all the old familiar roads but unfortunately not with the old familiar person! This morning, after Mass, Winifred Jackson (nee Lugg) said 'Bobs' thought I might like to go to the sea with them this afternoon, so I thought I might as well. Mamma and Baby, Winifred and 'Bobs' and then myself comprised the party. Oh, my darling, you would have loved it so, it really does look beautiful now, I kept feeling so SORRY all the time that you couldn't be seeing everything – the cloud effects were lovely, "Than these November skies, Is no sky lovelier," and Dorset with "its bare wind-swept hills" looked at its best with great patches of brown bracken tucked on the hills and Golden Cap – shining not quite so golden because you were not there. It brought last winter very vividly back to me, we even passed the cross-roads just outside Lyme where we turned down to our favourite parking place. You know, although we wouldn't like a repetition, we had some lovely times last winter.

Do you remember one dark night at Lyme, when the sea was very rough, walking along the promenade? I can still hear the suck and roll of the pebbles and see the spray flung up in the lamp light.

Or another calm, moonlit night when we walked to the end of the Cobb and there was no-one else in the world but the two of us? A little time must pass before one realises how fully one has enjoyed these things.

I have just been thinking how full of events these parts have been for us – I saw Portland, Lambert's Castle too, each has its particular memory. I shall love them for as long as I shall love you – always.

But this is merely or really all that went on right inside me. On the surface I was observing and seeing things. Darling, it is a desperate mistake for a young, newly-married couple to have a parent living with them. Poor Mrs Lugg, my heart broke for her. Obviously 'Bobs' nearly drives her insane. It has got to the point where he really gets on her nerves and she could happily murder him. He is self-willed, argumentative, slightly selfish and irritating, but so are all men! In Winifred's eyes it is almost part of his charm. She says he is hopeless but loves him for it, or in spite of it. But poor Mrs Lugg is so much older that she finds it difficult to bear his fecklessness. Actually I found that he improves on acquaintance, though he is not the sort of man I should like to marry. He is too boyish and irresponsible. Oh, there are such lots of things I want to tell you about them all. It is so interesting being the observer and seeing where the mistakes are and that it really is nobody's fault but is just that it is all wrongly arranged.

You know that it is such a NUISANCE, apart from anything else, not having you here near me to tell you everything.

One thing I must say, though – Winifred was saying how opposites seem to attract one another; she said, "I was thinking it was the same with you and Mr Connolly. He seems so quiet and you are so lively." I have just been thinking though – you know how I used to think we were so different – now I don't, not half so much, you are not quiet really, I am not lively really. We are a bit of each and the same as each other. Anyhow I adore you, you are the nicest man on earth – we are going to get married, work hard, pray hard and be tremendously happy.

And now I refuse to be Juliet-ish and linger over my goodnights, though goodness knows it is nearly as hard as leaving the real you.

I have had such a nice talk with you. I wonder if you have had one with me, a really nice long one? It is a consolation when you don't feel too deep in the dumps. Goodnight and God Bless You, My darling.

Monday. Good morning, my pet. I had seven heart attacks this morning before breakfast in case there would be no letter from you – but you saved my life.

What did you do on Saturday and Sunday? You did not tell me.

About next weekend: Saturday is the Jumble sale and the Jacksons have asked me around again on Sunday, so that I shall not mind really if you do not come. Besides it will hardly be worth it, since the clocks go – whichever way they do go – next week-end, and if you came on Sunday we would have no time together. I am also very doubtful about coming to Frome. Getting back at about 11.00a.m. on Monday (even though it is very kind of Mrs Bird to offer to put me in the spare room) would mean that there would be three music lessons missed and I don't know when I could make them up. Besides, I don't imagine Mother Superior would exactly rave about the idea. However, it remains to be considered, I'll see. I must say goodbye before this gets too Monday morning-ish – otherwise it's rather a nice letter, don't you think?

Lots of Love,
Noreen.

TODAY, CECIL AND NOREEN are sitting out on the patio. A rare event, since the start of winter. During summer and autumn, they had greatly enjoyed coming outside, into the open air. The leaves have gone from the giant beech trees, but the cedars stay green all year and the lawn is wide and restful to the eye. They watch the birds, the sparrows and coal-tits, and the robins, and the flock of starlings which, all through the summer, used to swoop in to scour the lawn for whatever it was they preyed upon so avidly, when the gardener had finished cutting the grass with his petrol-powered mower. Today the air is sharp but the sky so clear it is almost white, and the sun, low in the sky, is dazzling.

Noreen is sitting on a wooden bench, just beyond the conservatory where they sit when it rains. Cecil's chair is drawn up alongside, facing the lawn.

"It is really quite warm in the sun. You wouldn't think it was February would you, darling?" Noreen stands and then takes a few paces to the edge of one of the flowerbeds. She admires the splash of yellow made by some early daffodils against the brown earth.

Cecil has been rather sluggish recently, Noreen thinks. It will do him good, coming out here. Buck him up a bit. She sits back down. Composes herself, her hands resting together in her lap.

"It was a day like this, I made that journey to the Holy Isle of Iona, before we were engaged," Cecil says suddenly, in a surprisingly loud voice. "1937, I think it was. It may have been in June or July, but it was really bright like this."

"Oh, yes, I'd forgotten you did that. What a wonderful adventure!"

"Covered the first three hundred miles in two days. Yes... oh, yes. Up through the Vale of Evesham... and on to Shropshire. Stayed overnight somewhere... in Market Drayton, where I was born, if I remember rightly. I was born there, wasn't I?..."

"Market Drayton, that's right darling."

"Then I pressed on until I reached Chester... skirted Liverpool and got up as far as Blackpool. Goodness knows why. Ah, yes... spent the night there. That's right... left the car with my aunt in Blackpool and took a train for the remainder of the journey. Through the hills of Westmorland and Cumberland, past Carnforth and Oxenholme, over Shap, funny name that, isn't it... Shap? Over Shap to somewhere and somewhere. That was it... to Penrith and Carlisle, and then Gretna Green. I remember evening drawing in, passing conifers, empty river beds, oak trees, stone walls... can't for the life of me remember where we were then. I didn't see Glasgow, because it was dark by then, but, with the dawn, Oban came into view."

"Wow!"

"Wow?"

"Oban coming into view."

"Well, yes, it was. Wow. So what was next? Oh, yes. It was onto the good ship 'King George', between all these little islands in the Firth of Lorne, around the south-westerly point of Mull and soon, soon... what do you think I saw, Noreen?"

"The Isle of Wight?"

"Don't tease me, no, it was... I've forgotten now! What was it? Ummm... The Orkneys... The Hebrides... No... That was it... the Isle of Iona. Have I mentioned it is famous for its association with the great saint, Saint Columba? Have I already said that?"

"No, darling."

"And would you have any idea how much that trip cost me? A trip of about twelve hundred miles lasting ten days?"

"No idea at all, darling?"

"Seven pounds! I am sure it was only seven... for my food, accommodation, petrol train fares, boat fares..."

"Well, well... the cost of one meal today."

"Y'em... How about that?" Cecil smiles shyly at Noreen. Then he inhales deeply and, using his armrests as support, pushes himself up, almost to a standing position.

"Oooops! That's very good, darling. But you should be careful, you mustn't try that without help from the staff."

They sit for a little longer. Cecil's eyelids begin to droop. Noreen pushes the chair inside the house. By the time they have ascended in the lift and returned to Cecil's room, the blanket of warmth indoors has caused Cecil to drowse. His head lolls forward.

THE NEXT TIME Cecil looks up he is in his room, alone. He can see a reddish glow through the window. A sunset. He can hear the rattle of teaspoons in saucers coming from down the corridor outside, but otherwise all is peaceful. He reaches for his box of letters. A pang of sadness enters his heart as he notices the pile of those unread is shrinking fast.

He always thinks of Noreen as smiling and laughing, constant and dependable. Yet it was not always like that. Looking back, he realises that she had her difficult times, just as much as he – maybe more so, he thinks; it was just that he did not see it like that at the time. He had felt that if he really believed that something was straightforward, it would be. He felt it was important to keep things simple. Even when it came to their feelings for each other. When Noreen talked about her feelings, his worry was that analysing things, looking into them too deeply, risked damaging them in some way, and his great fear was that repairing things might be beyond him, if ever they went wrong.

Her next letter had worried him so much. He had felt powerless to do anything to make things better and had simply carried on as usual, in the hope that she would come out of it. Looking back, he feels that Noreen was unhappy about something. He has no idea what. She talked a lot about her father at the time. She loved him profoundly, and yet she always felt she had to be as strong as him; and for his part, her father did not like other people to be stronger than him. And, come to think of it, he had talked a lot about his own father to her at that time, too.

My Dearest Cecil,

Since you have ordered me to write to you for Monday morning – me voilà. Though goodness knows what I am going to say.

I have felt so queer this week – terribly depressed at times and yet (don't get alarmed) I have hardly thought about you at all – I mean I have not had that heart-breaking longing for you. If I did think about you, it was as if you were someone I had known a long, long time ago, someone outside myself. It's a very unpleasant feeling – but this evening at Benediction I got a bit 'closer' to you because I suddenly thought of you being in Yeovil and imagined you at the meeting of the Knights of Saint Columba and envied Mr Woods and Mr (Oh blow, the man we saw in the Lyme Regis Cafe) and Miss O'Neil's husband – any news of her by the way? Were they all pleased to see you? Tell me all about it in your next letter.

Yesterday I did nothing except go to the Doctor and to see 'The Mikado'. I rejoice to say that I have not got appendicitis – the Doctor says it is a spot of inflammation and he's given me some medicine to cure it – I had the same thing about eighteen months ago, only on the other side.

'The Mikado' was very good. Margaret came with me and we saw 'Bobs' Jackson as large as life and as still as a statue several times. I forget the name of the part he took. The colours were very beautiful – subdued but rich.

I wonder did you have any luck with the house – I am longing to know and yet I dread it – I have hardly dared to think of it, yet I think of it all the time? Somehow I have great faith in our getting it.

I am sorry this letter is a bit less than effusive but I can only write what I feel. You would not want me to be insincere would you? I love you all the time, only sometimes it can be expressed, while at other times – like now – all I feel for you is inexpressible. I can only tell you again that I love you for always.

God bless you, my dear love,

Noreen.

By the following weekend, Noreen had rediscovered something much more like her usual feelings. Cecil remembers his relief.

From My Bed
Saint Gildas' Convent,
Chard.
Sunday 10th December, 1939.

My Dearest Love,

You have been so close to me tonight and I have been so very happy that I wanted to talk to you a little longer before I went to sleep. I have just been praying so very hard for you and for your intention – that is the great consolation with prayer, it is never wasted, so that, even if you do not get what you want, my prayers will be there in heaven waiting to be used for you in a way which God knows is best.

Do you know, tonight I had such a big 'think' that I wanted to tell you – it was just that I had a sudden and very real conviction that it will always be alright with us because our love is founded on such a sure base – on our Faith.

Whatever differences in character we may have, they are so little and unimportant when we have such a great and precious thing in common.

Earlier, I was reading the copy of the Catholic Herald you gave me. There was an article on the life of Saint Elizabeth of Hungary. It impressed me very much because I realised that human love in no way lessens our Divine love, rather does it intensify it. The article said that Elizabeth was able to put the whole of Ludwig (her husband) into her heart because it was Christ's Heart – she loved him as a normal woman loves (she cried – 'All joy and all the world are dead to me!' at his death, and became almost crazed with grief) and yet she became a Saint. Of course she did great work for the poor and sick in her own country, spent long hours in prayer throughout the night, and on the death of her husband became a member of The Third Order of Saint Francis. Heard of it? Apparently it's an association which started in the thirteenth century. Members were bound by rule to dress more soberly, fast more strictly, pray more regularly, hear Mass more frequently, and practice works of mercy more systematically than ordinary persons living in the world. They were called the Brothers and Sisters of Penance of Saint Francis. Wow!

Today, too, I read some words the priest says at the end of a marriage service – "Remember that no man can love his wife enough if he love not God more; and no woman can love her husband enough unless she love God more..." So we have a lot of hard spiritual work to do, haven't we?

I know that I am not half grateful enough to God for all He has given me – you will have to thank Him sometimes for me.

And now I must say goodnight. I am afraid I have been rather serious but I do hope I have not been 'preachy', I do not mean to be.

Pray often for me that I may be fit and worthy to be your wife when you need me – you see how fearlessly I say it, and how I tell you all my deepest 'thinks', so now you cannot doubt that I love you.

God bless you and keep you always,
Noreen.

Noreen tells him to pray, so that she may be fit to be his wife, when Cecil had not felt fit to be Noreen's husband.

One fault which had often intruded on their happiness was his need to be sure about things, rather than to trust to instinct, he thinks. Like that time she encouraged him to apply for promotion to London. Deep down he believed he could have done that job. But his annual assessment at the time had said he needed a 'reasonable period of time' in order for him to 'consolidate the projects' he had 'in train'. Mister Brown must have had good reason for his assessment, he had felt. Because of Brown's experience, he had allowed himself to be guided into inertia when he might have progressed earlier.

Noreen managed to keep looking forward, even when she felt frustrated and depressed. Cecil finds another letter which Noreen sent him before Christmas that year.

Saint Gildas' Convent,
Chard.
Thursday 14th December, 1939.

My Dearest Cecil,

Something happened to me last night – and I think it was partly due to Mary Bennett.

It is rather difficult to explain but suddenly, in bed last night, I saw how silly, futile and unnecessary it is for us to go on waiting, house or no house, stern parent or no stern parent! I just sort of KNEW that it was right for us to get married soon. I suddenly didn't mind a tiny bit what Mother or Daddy said, and felt quite ready to accept any consequences which might follow.

And this is how I think it was partly due to Mary Bennett. She came to see me last night and she was telling me that she is having a pretty hard time at home. Among other things, her father objects to her being friendly with the boyfriend – her father says after all they have spent on her she should only think about a Career, that her parents have always been enough for her, why does she want other male company, their whole life has been devoted to her and many such familiar arguments.

And, afterwards, when she had gone, it suddenly occurred to me that mine is not an exceptional case but that all parents are like that, at least "only child" parents who have been very close to their children.

I mean to a great extent I think Mother and Daddy cannot get used to the idea that they are not the primary consideration in my life – they still think that YOU are secondary, it is just lack of realisation that makes them take this attitude – Oh! I can't explain it, it's no good, perhaps I'll try when we see each other.

However I feel wonderfully relieved to feel like this. It almost seems to make the house not matter half so much. Though of course I should like it because once we have a place to live, there will be, as you often say, more chance of us ALL being happy.

Darling you must do whatever you think best. Don't THINK about my liking it or not wanting to be poor or anything like that. The only thing I want is you and for you to be happy. So if you want me to go and live in a cellar with you – I'll come even if there are rats, mice and other vermin.

It seems imperative that I see you before I go home, so if I don't get a summons to Frome on Saturday what about if I come to Frome on Wednesday, or even Tuesday if I could wangle it, and stay until Thursday, on my way home for the Christmas hols. In fact, come to think of it, I'd rather do that than come this weekend, if you don't mind. I could get to Frome from Bristol and then go back to Bristol and go on home. What do you think?

It's getting late, I must get this in the post.

Goodbye my darling and Good luck.

All My Love,

Noreen.

They had decided Noreen was quite right. They would marry. Cecil found his trepidation dissolved once they had got together and finally and irrevocably made their decision, over a Frome teacake. They had never been happier, he recalls; their decision made, their future bright, and all the practical arrangements yet to be negotiated.

He would be a married man. He liked the sound of that, he recalls. It resonated with a status which being a 'bachelor' would never achieve. There was a completeness about it. They would marry on the 27th of February, they had decided, the date Jack Byrne himself had originally suggested. He would hardly be able to argue with that, they had thought.

Noreen's joy and enthusiasm had certainly matched his own, at that time, he remembers, as was evident by the energy she suddenly put into her shopping trips to Liverpool's big stores! Cecil looks at the Real Photogravure Letter Card Noreen sent him from Liverpool, the day after she had got home to Rhosllanerchrugog. There are several joined sepia views of Liverpool affixed to a sturdy brown envelope, with 'British Production Throughout' proudly printed on the outside of the envelope. A quality product, that has lasted sixty years, Cecil muses. On the back of the views of Liverpool, Noreen had managed to fill every inch of the space designated for writing.

Lewis's,
Liverpool.
Friday, 22nd December, 1939.

My Dearest,
I am with Mother on the balcony of Lewis's Ranelagh Restaurant. Mother has treated me to tea and having consumed a thousand egg and cress sandwiches and therefore being unable to attack my sherry trifle for the moment,

I have decided to drop you a line. But I doubt whether I shall be intelligible as the band is 'swinging' – Alexander's Rag Time Band, and Mother's comments on the whole scene before us are bound to interrupt me.

From here, there is a marvellous view of the hordes of vessels going up and down the River Mersey and of the back yards of Liverpool's shops (!) – the tugs are pottering about everywhere and the huge cranes of Cammel Laird's look rather grim.

Do you know I am a physical wreck after a positive orgy of shopping – but I have got what I wanted – which is what usually happens.

I am expecting a letter from you in the morning so I shall reply properly to that, if it arrives alright. Postcards and letter cards are handy little things but not terribly satisfying to the recipients, are they?

Mother has just said she wishes you were here with us; she is enjoying herself tremendously buying clothes for HERSELF in between stops for teas, coffees and more tea. Ah, well... back to the sherry trifle! Goodbye, my lamb. Keep Well. You would love driving through The Mersey Tunnel, I just know it. See the picture of the tunnel entrance taken from the museum steps, on the other side of this?

All My Love,
Noreen.

His own Christmas had been quieter, though he retains one recollection of driving into Bristol one Saturday and purchasing a white sheepskin rug from a shop in Clifton. He had fallen in love with its softness and thought it would be the perfect thing for Noreen to step onto, when she got out of bed in the mornings. It had been his main Christmas present for Noreen and he had kept it back, to give to her as a surprise, after Christmas. She had written to him again, the day after her shopping spree in Liverpool, before his own letter reached her.

Darling,

I do hope this will be in time to wish you a very happy Christmas – may it be the last we ever have to spend apart. You will be glad to hear that Daddy has responded quite well to my ultimatum about the 27th February 1940 as THE date. We are still speaking anyway!

I am consoling myself during this time without you with a thousand happy memories, but I look forward to the time when reality will take their place, when I shall have you for my very, very own and I shall be your very, very own. Oh darling, we shall be so happy.

All My Love,
Noreen.

ॐ

DURING CHRISTMAS 1939, time passed for Cecil more slowly than it had ever done before. He spent a few days, including Christmas Day, with his parents down in Chard, but for most of the Christmas period he was in Frome and at work. There were letters to write for the wedding, and he continued to look for a suitable property for himself and Noreen, but Noreen's letters were the highlight of his day.

Norland,
15, Clive Road
Rhosllanerchrugog.
Thursday, 28th December, 1939.

My Dearest Cecil,

It is such an age since I saw you or wrote (five whole days ago – my last letter!) that you seem a million miles and a million years away, although your letter of yesterday did make you seem more real. Do you know I only got it yesterday, the 27th, and you had posted it on the 22nd, so I feared you would not get my parcel before you returned to Frome. I am so sorry, but I suppose your mother will forward it.

It is almost impossible to 'talk' to you properly as Mother has been chattering away to me since I started. I just made an impassioned appeal for silence and NOW she is conducting a very one-sided conversation with the bird, Joey. "Pretty Joey, Pretty Joey..." If she says it once more, I shall scream! Whoops, not very charitable that... and she the woman who brought me into the world!

Outside, the garden is looking somewhat unfamiliar under a thick coat of snow. It was snowing when we got up this morning and it has not stopped yet.

We went over to Aunt Sarah's on Christmas Day and

stayed until the next evening – I was terribly lonely for you, especially on Christmas Night when I went to bed! It was probably because Mother, Aunt Sarah and I had to sleep three in a bed, and my Aunt Sarah had the hare-brained idea that we should sleep side by side crossways in the bed. Of course we had to sleep with our knees under our chins to keep any bedclothes on us, except when we felt too cramped, and then we'd stretch our feet into the wide open spaces only withdrawing them when the cold became too penetrating. It was rather fun. We laughed a good deal but got practically no sleep, so that is how I longed for you in the fastness of the night...

Yesterday we had some friends in to tea, Mr and Mrs Kelly, and they stayed all the evening, and today our neighbour, Mrs Howarth, has asked us in to tea – so that we can "have a good old chat..." Oh, crumbs! So you see how difficult it is for me to find TIME to do anything.

Incidentally, Mother has invited my Aunt and Uncle, two cousins, and Simone and Frank, and another Uncle up here for the day, on Sunday – so that I think it would NOT be a very good idea for you to come this weekend, since we are so pressed for time and will need it all for discussion and since it would also probably be more convenient for you. I know it is really too late to be telling you this. If it is, then I suppose we'll just have to put up with it.

Yesterday I over-heard Daddy telling Mr Kelly about 'us' and saying what a very nice fellow you were and singing your praises very highly. I smiled to myself because I thought that somehow the two of you, in spite of grave differences of opinion, do seem to have developed a mutual respect for each other.

In spite of the freezing weather, I have decided that ours shall be a white wedding so you can get your necessaries as soon as you like.

I really cannot solve the furniture problem. My feeling is that it would be best to go to Liverpool to get essentials – I am going to do some more shopping there next week, probably Tuesday, so I'll get some catalogues and things if you like.

Thank you for the chocs. I thought it was sweet of you to send them, as if you haven't given me enough. I have not bought your Christmas present yet. I am leaving it until we go to Liverpool.

By the way, could you please send me a list of people you want to invite to the wedding, because we'll need to be getting the invitations sent out before too long.

I have a dozen letters I ought to write, so perhaps I had better say goodbye. Mother said something about putting in a word to you, so I'll leave some room on the back of this page.

God Bless You, My Love,

Soon to be yours, really and truly yours,

Noreen.

On the back, Cecil's future mother-in-law had written a short letter to him.

My Dear Cecil,

Thank you ever so much for the lovely chocolates, it was so good of you to think of us both. We are looking forward to seeing you soon. Hope you had a nice time at home over the Christmas holiday and that both your parents are keeping well.

All best wishes,

Kitty Byrne.

Cecil had been pleased with the house which he found in Frome. A detached, three-bedroomed property, with a dignified double bay window at the front. In Windsor Crescent. Convenient for town, yet not hemmed in by other properties. Fireplaces in the living room and the lounge, which heated the water, and more fireplaces in two of the bedrooms. A modern cooker and a well equipped bathroom upstairs. A long drive on which he was able to park the car, and at the rear a large garden where he would cultivate vegetables and plant fruit bushes, to help them cope with food rationing. It was a property of some stature and yet the rental was well within what they could afford. Ample space for himself and Noreen, and room to raise a family if one came along, he had thought. It had been worth all the hours searching to secure them a suitable home, when he read Noreen's next letter. Noreen had already resigned from her teaching post at Saint Gildas' Convent and was living with her parents, but had been so excited at the news she had not had the composure to write her address at the top of the letter. He had received it in January, 1940.

Sunday.

My Darling Cecil,

I simply don't know what to do with myself, I am so happy – it's unbelievable. I simply ooze happiness. I can feel it spilling out of my eyes – I want to dance and shout and laugh – I wish you were with me. Thank you so much for your wire and then your letter – the house sounds absolutely PERFECT for us.

It is going to mean a great deal of work to get it all furnished, but I can't wait to get started. I was passing A. J. Rowlands & Sons in Wrexham the other day and noticed they sell 'black-out fabrics' – blue, green, brown, black – all absolutely opaque and needing no lining, for one and six a yard, the 34 inch wide piece, and three shillings a yard, the 48 inch wide piece. Perhaps you could measure the windows, if you have any cause to go to the house in the near future?

On a less happy note, Mother was suffering from a slight bilious attack yesterday morning and it got worse throughout the day. I had to put her to bed with hot water bottles and lots more blankets. Since there was no brandy in the house, I staggered through the black-out down to the local public house and caused a minor commotion when I walked into the bar and demanded brandy. But everyone was very charming and most polite and made no attempt to take advantage of a beautiful defenceless maiden! That was yesterday. I have just been up to her and she seems a bit brighter. I date her rallying from the time she consumed those tiny sips of brandy which I took up yesterday evening. She was so extremely refined in the way she sipped it – her lip trembled delicately over the rim of the glass for ages before she took any brandy – but I am convinced it gave her heart, whether or not it really had any medicinal value!

Thank you for sending the list of people you want to invite to the reception. I will get invitations sent off as soon as possible. So far nearly everyone I have invited has accepted, so it looks as though there are going to be simply hordes there. By the way, I think it was a brilliant idea of yours to hold the ceremony in the Catholic Pro Cathedral in Wrexham. It will add just that little touch of grandeur to the occasion, making it all the more memorable. We are going to arrange the reception in a private hotel near to the Church – The Carlton, in Grosvenor Road. I am sure you will like it.

I had better bring this letter to a close now as Daddy is looking hungry for his supper, so I must feed him and, incidentally, myself and leave you once again.

I await with great impatience your next letter and further instructions. I have packed most of my things and anything I have been unable to fit in I shall be leaving with Mummy and Daddy for the time being.

God has been very good to us, hasn't He? It has been worth all the fed-upness to feel like this again.

Goodbye, my darling. Look after yourself and don't catch this dreaded 'flu which everybody seems to be getting – I want you to be as fit as a fiddle, on the big day. A thousand kisses.

Noreen.

*

Cecil had felt a little out of things, being so far away, and not having previously made the acquaintance of many of the relatives whom Noreen was inviting. But his main worry had been what he was going to do about getting a Best Man. His thoughts stray back over some of the old friends he made in Chard and Frome. In a sense, the fact that they had been *old* friends had been part of the problem, he recalls. They had all been much older than him, the friends he made in the Knights of Saint Columba, the League of Nations and the Civil Service Catholic Guild – and it had been complicated by the fact that most of his friends amongst the membership of the Civil Service Catholic Guild had been women. The few school friends with whom he still corresponded were away on active service and unavailable. For the first time in many years he had been acutely aware just how little control he had over what was happening. He could no longer order things howsoever he wished. Things were being decided without him even knowing about them, let alone having a say about what the decision should be. It was true, he recalls, it was he who had suggested that the Catholic Pro Cathedral would be a magnificent place to hold the wedding ceremony, but at that time he had had absolutely no idea what The Carlton would be like for the reception – where he would have to stand to make his speech, how friendly or otherwise the proprietors might be, how crowded with other people the room might be, or whether it would be just right – and, because he had never been there before, as soon as he got there he would even have to make enquiries as to where the gentlemen's lavatories were, which was a perfect example of the sort of thing he would have far preferred not to have had to worry about at that stage of the proceedings.

Noreen had been quick to understand how he felt. Had given him the feeling that they were going through it all together. That he was not alone any more.

Norland,
15, Clive Road,
Rhosllanerchrugog.
Tuesday, 23rd January, 1940.

My Dearest Cecil,

Thank you, darling, for your most recent 'missive', which I have just finished reading – there are some unhappy parts in it, I know, but it is always lovely to hear from you.

Yet I am still left rather disturbed about you, I wish you would not be in the dumps. I have been thinking about it and your regrets at having lost the first careless rapture, and all connected with our wedding not turning out exactly as you had dreamed and planned. Is it THAT which makes you miserable? Anyway, darling, what does it MATTER? It is only the things in life that really MATTER that really count. A lot of obstacles, some misery and a lot of unpleasantness – they don't make any difference to US. Actually they are probably a very good preparation for marriage. In a very little time we shall be able to look back and see them in their true perspective, not magnified as we see them now.

I was thinking the other night of the seriousness of this step – we are both on the threshold of a new life with all that we have built up in the old life within us – both good and evil. And I was wondering whether together we will go on making a stronger and greater propensity for good grow within us, whether we will be able to see only the GOOD in each other and suppress the evil inclinations within ourselves. With God's help we will, but it is not going to be easy. I suppose, my own, that you are quite, quite sure that you want to marry me – you are sure that you have not built up an idealistic picture or set an impossible standard? I am afraid that you might have done that and that you will be disappointed.

But I think that perhaps I am being unduly alarmed. I always expected that before I was married I should be beset by a thousand doubts and fears. Well, there aren't a thousand, but I sometimes have some. There are times when you annoy me, times when you worry me, but I realise how little they mean, how petty I am to notice them when there are such great and lovely moments, as on our last weekend together during my visit to Chard, when I felt the great fullness of your love. Please God I will never prove unworthy of it. The other evening at Benediction, I was trying to think how I could best be worthy of you and, looking at the Blessed Sacrament, I knew that the only way was to be worthy in the eyes of God – if we are true to Him, He will never desert us.

Goodbye, my dearest. Pray hard for me.

Noreen.

There was not too much time to have many more doubts, Cecil recalls. He was still in Frome through the early weeks of February, hard at work at the office and spending as much time as possible decorating the house, putting up bookshelves, and installing various pieces of furniture which he managed to acquire. Then there were the regular weekly stints with his Catholic organisations, visits to his parents, and, by no means least, the honeymoon to organise.

They had set their hearts on a honeymoon in London. After the wedding, they would drive down to spend one night in the house in Frome and the next morning drive on to London.

As the wedding date had approached, he had increasingly felt life passing in a blur, but he had been determined to look after his newly-wed wife with every fibre of his being and, if necessary, every drop of his blood. One of the last tasks he completed before heading north to the wedding was to lay in an emergency store of food in their new house, to cater for unexpected eventualities of any sort. In one large cardboard box, he gathered tins of pilchards, herrings, sardines, Lyle's syrup, butter beans, peas, soup, Ovaltine, Cocoa, Chocolate, evaporated milk, beef gelatin, corned beef, brisket beef, crabmeat, treacle and tomatoes. In another cardboard box, he collected two cartons of Spry, 21 candles, half a pound of rice, a pound of milk chocolate, a dozen dried eggs, five pounds of soap, one jar of honey, a pound of starch, five boxes of England's Glory matches and two bottles of lemonade.

A few days before Cecil set out to travel to North Wales for the wedding, he received a final letter from Noreen.

Norland,
15, Clive Road
Rhosllanerchrugog.
Monday, 19th February, 1940.

My dearest Cecil,

Just one or two quick things. I need to know how many people you want to send wedding cake to – because I am buying the little boxes to put it in, as soon as I know. It was something I thought Mummy had dealt with but it turns out she thought I had it on my list of things to do! Anyway, could you give it some thought so that you can let me know when you come up?

One other thing, are we travelling down to Frome after the wedding next Tuesday, or shall we be leaving it to the Wednesday? Also, how long will we be staying in Frome, because if it's anything more than a flying visit, we shall need some provisions and I shall need to get them on Saturday, because there will be no time on Monday?

Oh, yes, a little while back, you mentioned a programme for Monday "because we shall be very busy". What doing, please? I must know because I am afraid I shall be very occupied and there is no time left for anything else – I have an appointment with the hairdresser in the morning, I want to get everything absolutely ready for the next day – and if you knew the pressing of the dress that will be required, checking this, checking that, tacking a hem here and letting down a sleeve there, you'd be sorry for me, you've never seen Mother à la dressmaker mode – then, Mother has to go to the hairdressers in the afternoon, while I stay to receive my aunt and two of my cousins who will be arriving. So that if there is anything very pressing that we must attend to, it will have to be between about midday and 1.30p.m.

BAD NEWS – Jim cannot get the 27th off to be your best man. Mother is going to Ellesmere tomorrow and, if you wish, she could ask one of my cousins, Billy, if he can do it – a messy arrangement having a best man you've not even seen. I'm not really too keen on having Billy; he's much too young for the job, only eighteen, and he has no striped trousers or black coat, but we would have to put up with that. He does have a very nice navy suit, but it is not quite the thing – will you mind?

Talking of suits, would you bring your navy blue suit for going away? Your plus fours are really rather shabby and, truly, my sweet, you will find that navy will go perfectly with your overcoat.

I have made the appointment for the photos at Algernon Smith's in Wrexham – though I got a shock when I asked how much they'd be and the assistant said fifty five shillings a dozen, that is cabinet size. Let me know what you think of this – is it too dear? Though of course we won't want a dozen that size. How many do you think we'll want?

We shall also have to buy a present for the bridesmaid and the organist, I fear – I thought a bracelet for my cousin, May, the bridesmaid, and a box of chocs for Flo (the organist). Perhaps we had better get them on Monday?

Sorry, I have not had time to go to The Carlton Hotel yet to book your rooms for the Monday night, but I'm sure they'll have vacancies. I seem to have no time to breathe from morn till night. I am writing this very rapidly at 9.30 at night, my first free moment.

By the way, I hope I shall not be prey to rheumatism when you arrive. I spent half last night in bed in company with a leaking hot water bottle. When I woke up I had to swim for it very nearly.

Father Mortlake wrote from Tewkesbury to ask if we would like a tea or dinner service. I shall write to say tea, since you are not here to be consulted – if you would prefer a dinner service you could 'phone him and let me know when you see me – but Mother and Daddy want to give us a dinner service.

Mrs Howarth came in yesterday with a very lovely table cloth for us.

We had a very light fall of snow for about twenty minutes yesterday but since then it has been quite fine, sunny and dry but extremely cold. I shall probably freeze to death on Tuesday. I have bought a white velvet cloak to wear during the Wedding Mass but it is not a very adequate exchange for woollen jumpers. Don't worry, everyone says excitement will keep me warm – so see you excite me!

I must say goodnight now, darling. I think I am too busy even to be thrilled about the great day. I just feel that I shall be glad when it is all over, at the moment anyhow.

Mother is clamouring for my attention, reckoning who's coming and who isn't, so goodnight and God Bless.

It's a fine thought though, isn't it? By Tuesday next week, I shall be Mrs Connolly, please God – unless I change my mind – Heaven forbid!

Big kiss and love,
Noreen.

THE RIGHT REVEREND Monsignor G. Nightingale stood at the foot of the altar steps and smiled at the congregation. He was a kindly old priest with snow-white hair.

"Before we start," he had said, "I'd just like to say a few words, especially to those of you who have travelled a long way to come to the wedding. I know we have had a light fall of snow overnight – I can hear all your teeth rattling from here, even those of you at the back, but I've some good news... I've just been listening to the weather forecast on the radio and we'll be having no more snow for a day or two. And I *know* that nothing can dispel the warmth we all hold in our hearts for this brave, young couple who have come here today to pledge themselves to each other in our presence."

Cecil had often wondered why the Monsignor had described himself and Noreen as 'brave'. Perhaps it had something to do with choosing to get married at that time of year, or perhaps it was because the war was on and the future was therefore so much more uncertain than it had been in peacetime. Anyhow, it had provided a human touch and set the tone for the day. Monsignor Nightingale had known Noreen and her family through Noreen's links with the Convent in Wrexham, and had treated Cecil as if he had known him all his life, even though they had met only just before the service began.

Cecil was feeling a lot happier by the Tuesday morning, he recalls. Noreen's cousin, Jim, had finally been able to arrange to take time off work to be his Best Man. A civil servant, like himself, Cecil had felt confident that Jim would do a good job. And he had done an excellent job, Cecil is sure, apart from referring to "Noreen's inextinguishable love for Eric" at one point in his speech, before hastily correcting himself with the words, "... for Cecil", and pretending a sudden cough had caused him to mis-pronounce Cecil's name. Jim had been dressed in an appropriate jacket, trousers and waistcoat, and had even sported an impressive gold watch-chain, Cecil remembers, as well as a pristine white shirt with a silver tie, like himself, so that in the end Cecil's fear that his Best Man would be a juvenile, who had just graduated to wearing long trousers, was not realised.

Noreen had looked radiant. The cold weather, though it had been inconvenient, had given a fresh glow to her cheeks which had contrasted with her alabaster skin and shimmering silk dress and had given her the appearance of a precious piece of porcelain. Having processed down the aisle to Flo's stirring rendition of Wagner's Wedding-March, her hand resting lightly on Jack Byrne's arm, Noreen had paused beside Cecil's bench and he had then turned towards her, feeling that everything in the universe at that moment could not be more right. Noreen was the woman he loved. His bride. Not a fantasy figure or a mannequin in a bridal store window. The real thing.

Not normally quick to find the right words where emotions were concerned, on this occasion he had experienced an overwhelming desire to put his feelings into words. As they paused momentarily, side by side, before taking their places at their respective kneelers, he had whispered in Noreen's ear, "Well done... Well done!"

The service had been completed without a hitch. The exchange of rings had been facilitated by the fact that their hands were so cool their fingers were not in the least swollen. After taking the vows, Cecil had knelt on his kneeler assuming he would feel different. He was now a married man. He found he felt exactly the same physically as he had ten minutes before, apart from a feeling of warmth which had spread across his chest, a kind of fullness which left him slightly breathless. Yet Cecil had seen that in agreeing to marry him, Noreen was giving him a priceless gift, all that she had to give – her very self. He prayed that her sacrifice would inspire him with a love for her that would never cease.

He had been very pleased with the rooms in The Carlton Hotel. The room his parents had been given was slightly larger than his own, but both rooms had a wash-hand basin and a small electric fire which gave out a very adequate heat. It had proved a great luxury, on the morning of the wedding, being able to shave in the room without having to queue for the bathroom, as he was used to doing in his lodgings in Frome. And he had been able to see the dining room at breakfast-time and prepare himself by picturing the proceedings which would be taking place there later in the day.

His speech had been prepared some weeks beforehand. Taking care to consult his book on *Etiquette For Formal Occasions* by Fortescue Albright, he had established that he would be responding with thanks, on behalf of his wife and himself, to everyone who had been involved in the organisation of the wedding, ending by proposing a toast to the bridesmaids, or bridesmaid as would be the case at their wedding. He had carefully established that his initial words should be addressed to those people present of the highest social standing, and should then extend to encompass all present. As there were not to be any Kings, Queens, titled people, Lord Mayors or Lady Mayoresses attending the reception, he deduced that senior male clergy should be the first acknowledged, then any members present of female Religious Orders, then the rest: "Right Reverend

Monsignor, Reverend Father (Father Mortlake, as unfortunately Father O'Beirne was not going to be able to make it), Mother Superior, Ladies and Gentlemen" – had seemed about right, and he had decided to pay tribute to the bridesmaid, May, by describing her as "more beautiful than the month of May itself". He had not met May, at the time of composing his speech, but Noreen had said she was very pretty so he determined to say it and to add their thanks for her "unceasing help and graceful presence throughout the whole of this wonderful day". On the whole, this had worked out quite well when he had looked back on it after the wedding. May had seemed suitably flattered and been delighted with the bracelet with which he presented her. It was only later he discovered that his future mother-in-law, Kitty, and May's mother did not get on very well because of some dispute years before, and Kitty had felt he had been far too effusive towards May – when it was Noreen he was marrying.

Once his speech was planned out, Cecil began to worry about what Jack would say, and whether he would say it correctly. The book said that Jack Byrne, as the bride's father, would have the task of making a speech immediately after the meal, a speech which should sum up his pleasure on this happy occasion and which would end with a toast proposed to the bride and groom. If his speech was inept or created the wrong atmosphere it would spoil it for the later speeches, he worried, however good they were. When Jack stood up and looked slowly around the room he had opened with the simple words, "I want to offer you all a very warm welcome here today, on behalf of Kitty and myself, and thank you all for coming..." In the body of his speech, there had been many more comments praising Noreen than praising him, Cecil had noticed. But Jack had gone on to describe him as "an upright man" and a man of "honour" and he had said that, if ever he had had a son, he would have been proud to have had a son like Cecil.

The section of the etiquette book which Cecil had enjoyed reading most was where it said, '...All that remains at the end of the reception is for the bride and groom to change. The best man announces their departure, the bride throws her bouquet into the throng, and the couple drive, or are driven away in a shower of confetti...' How earnestly he had looked forward to that moment. It had been regrettable that during their drive to Frome on that first evening they had to be accompanied by Pop and Mammy Connolly, at least as far as Bristol, but there had seemed little alternative. It had simply not made sense to leave them at the reception so that then they would have had to struggle back to Chard on the train on their own, when he and Noreen would be driving nearly all the way there, on their way to Frome. It had been a bit of a squash, Cecil recalls, fitting as many of their presents in as they could, but they had managed it. Noreen had not been happy about it – "I've married you, not your parents..." she had whispered after they had changed and got ready to leave, and he had told her what the plan was – but she had been exhausted after the tiring activity of the previous weeks and, once they had dropped his parents off at Bristol Station, she had started smiling a little more.

Cecil has found the list of the wedding presents and the people who gave them, at the bottom of his cashbox. He had typed the list up after the wedding, to help them organise their letters of thanks efficiently. He cannot resist counting the total number of presents, each time he looks at the list afresh. Sixty five. And eleven Greetings Telegrams in their faded gold envelopes.

He balances his spectacles on the end of his nose. Scans the list of gifts at random. None are large, many are still up at the house. Each one associated with someone involved with them in some way or another. The tea service from Father Mortlake, as promised. He had kept in touch, even after moving to Tewkesbury. A Wall Plaque of Our Lady from Monsignor Nightingale. "Tasteful", Noreen had called it. It had come from Italy. A set of Sherry Glasses from Father O'Beirne. An Electric Table Lamp from the Sisters and Pupils at Saint Gildas' Convent School, accompanied by a large Wall Crucifix from Mother Superior. And an Embroidered Tea Cloth from Sister Pauline (Children of Mary).

Yes, Jack and Kitty Byrne had presented them with the Dinner Service, tea towels and a set of bathroom towels – they had lasted for years. Cecil smiles at the other gift they received from Noreen's parents. He had forgotten all about it, perhaps understandably he thinks. A Box of Groceries. Jack had used his position as Manager at the Maypole to purchase a huge box of edible delicacies for them. Food rationing was the order of the day and Cecil, as a civil servant, had felt it would be more than his job was worth to accept this inappropriate gift. Only when Noreen had threatened to leave him, before they had even been married, had Cecil capitulated and agreed they could accept it.

His own parents had been equally generous. There had been the lovely Green Down Quilt and two Pairs of Blankets, two Pillow and Bolster Sets and Two Pairs of Sheets and Pillow Slips, as well as a Folkweave Spread and two Rugs which Mammy Connolly had made herself.

The rest had been generous to a fault, an Eight Day Clock from Mr Brown and Office Staff, Frome; an Oak Fruit Stand from the Maypole Staff, Wrexham; a Dinner Cloth from Robert Lester, their Bridesmaid's brother; a

Hand-Embroidered Bolster Set from May Lester, their Bridesmaid; a Linen Tea Cloth and Serviettes from Mr and Mrs F. Aplin; a Supper Cloth and Serviettes from Miss Russell and Mrs H. Pate; a Silver Butter Knife from Mrs Algernon Smith and Brenda – that was a nice touch, Cecil thinks, but only fair when the price of the wedding photographs is taken into account; a Holy Bible from Yeovil Council 285, that was from the Knights of Saint Columba, Cecil realises; a Vase from Miss Mullully; half a dozen Tea Knives from Mr and Mrs E. Hall; a Set of Cake Forks from Mr and Mrs T. Kelly from Liverpool; Egg Cups from Mrs J. Bird; a Set of Salad Servers from Mrs Galloway; a Clock from Mr and Mrs P. Doyle; a Cheese Dish from Sister de Chantal; a Cake Dish from Miss Williams and her fiancé; a Butter Dish and Stand from Mr G. Monslow; a Pickle Jar from Captain and Mrs E. Roberts; a Pale Rose Bedcover from Miss E. H. Ashworth, my aunt, thinks Cecil; a Pewter Tea Set from Mr J. Spellman; Cheese and Biscuits Dish from Misses Philly and Pat Balcombe; a Condiment Set from Mr J. Doyle, my Best Man; a Jam Dish from Mr. and Mrs. Harding; a Cheque from Miss Clare Kolb and Mr and Mrs J. Kolb; an Embroidered Table Cloth from Mr. and Mrs. H. Howarth; Broderie Anglaise from Mr and Mrs McBride, they would be Eric's parents, Cecil thinks. Noreen had told him that her father and Mr McBride had wanted her to marry Eric, but she had left it until many years later; a Hall Mirror and Brushes from Mr and Mrs H. Warburton; a Cheque from the Misses M. and H. Smith; a Supper Cloth from Mrs C. Tooth; a Wall Plate from Mr and Mrs H. Laurie; a Fruit Dish from Mr and Mrs W. Ellis; an Embroidered Tea Cloth from Mr and Mrs Cross; a Tea Cosy from Mrs Heath; a Set of Pyrex Dishes from Mrs Jones and Winnie; an Embroidered Trolley Set from Miss D. Herbert; a Luncheon Set from

Mr and Mrs F. Warburton; a Tray Cloth from Mr and Mrs Hopkins; a Supper Cloth and Serviettes from Miss M. Edwards; an Embroidered Settee Set from Sergeant and Mrs A. E. Doughty; a Pair of Fountain Pens from the Post Office Staff at Chard; a Fruit Bowl from Mr W. West; a Cut Glass Bowl from Mr and Mrs P. Smith; Table Mats from Mrs H. Galpin; a Picture from Mother Superior at The Convent in Wrexham and an Illuminated Address from the Convent Staff; a Table Cloth from Miss Thomas; a Coffee Percolator from Mrs Robinson; and a Brass Wall Plaque and Crumb Tray from Mrs M. White.

There were many more presents which were never put on the list, Cecil recalls. Presents from Noreen's relatives on the farm in Baltinglass and in Dublin, and from people who lived near his parents in Chard. Poor Mrs Lugg specially sent a bundle of miraculous Medals Of Our Lady with a note to say, "The enclosed medals have been actually on the Grotto in Lourdes, Wishing you every blessing and happiness in your future together." And then there were the telegrams. As Cecil replaces the wedding list and reaches for the telegrams, Noreen breezes in.

"HE... LLO...! What have you got there, Cecil?"

"Oh, just a few things..."

"What sort of things?"

"Ah, ye'm... Souvenir things..."

Cecil half-closes the box. Noreen sits beside him on the bed.

"May I see?"

Cecil leans back, resignedly. Sets the box on the top of his locker.

"I suppose you may, but it is not really of any interest to you."

Noreen moves over to the cashbox and leafs through a few of the telegrams, then suddenly throws back her head with a burst of explosive laughter.

"Do you remember our drive down to Bristol, after the wedding? We'd got your parents in the back of the car. I could just see the top of your mother's hat above the wedding presents which were piled on her lap, and I couldn't see your father at all! He was holding the box of groceries from Daddy, wasn't he, and the green down quilt on top of that, then, on top of everything, that table lamp with the enormous lamp-shade?"

"Yes, I remember that."

"And Pop kept saying, 'Well I'll go to Ffff...ishh...'"

"And I kept saying, 'Fishponds Pop? We're nearly there,' when we still had miles and miles to go before we got to Bristol! And you drove so slowly, like a mole making a new burrow, because it was so dark..."

"Ah, yes... that was because of the black-out, you see. I had to have covers on the headlights – just little slits for the beams of light, and they had removed the sign posts in case the Germans invaded, so it was a good job I knew the road quite well."

Noreen manages to stop laughing and opens one of the telegrams.

"'All Happiness From Mr and Mrs Flynn and Family'... It was a pity that the Flynns couldn't be at the wedding. Daddy would have liked Mr Flynn to come. They'd had to go to Ireland suddenly because her mother had died. Do you remember? They were that family who lived in Liverpool?"

Cecil shakes his head and then shifts as if he has just thought of something.

"Um... Just a minute. Was she the person who looked like Joan Bennett, and he the one who used to do an imitation of Josef Locke. I remember now, he told me all about how he had seen Josef Locke singing in Ireland before the war, when he was Josef McLaughlin?"

"No, no, that was the Murphys from Ponciau. They weren't invited."

"I don't remember then. The man I remember definitely sang like Josef Locke."

Noreen extracts from the box a small group photograph and studies it intently.

"My cousin, Frank, and Simone – don't they look young there?"

"Ah'em... They *were* young there."

"I know, I know. You look young there, too. Very handsome!"

"Six foot one."

"But not so proud of yourself that night!"

It comes back to Cecil in a rush. How he had bought some farm cider from a farmhouse just outside Bristol, at Almondsbury. The make-shift sign had read, 'BEST SCRUMPY 300 YARDS'. He had drunk hardly any champagne at the wedding because of the long drive ahead of him, he recalls, and although there had been funny moments in the car coming back there had been many tense moments too. So he had decided it would be a good time to try some farm-house cider. He had always wanted to try it. Something new on his wedding night.

"Oh, you *were* ill, Cecil! Remember?"

"Ah... y'em..."

"But you got up the next morning, to drive us both to London – as good as gold – even though you looked as green as the top of that water jug."

Noreen remembers him that morning putting one leg in his trousers and then having to run to the bathroom to be sick, with his other trouser leg and his braces dragging behind him along the floor. Her heart had gone out to him. Later, when she had asked him how he was feeling, he had said he felt just fine, absolutely fine, as if he had not been sick at all, and when they had sat down for breakfast he had tucked into the bacon, egg and black pudding, which she had extracted from the box of groceries, as if he had just returned from a brisk morning walk.

On that morning, they had driven from Frome to London for their honeymoon at the Strand Palace Hotel. Noreen had loved the hustle and bustle in the Strand, and everywhere that they went in London.

After booking in at the hotel on that first day, they had visited Westminster Cathedral to give thanks for their wonderful wedding the day before.

Noreen remembers the wedding as having had a dream-like quality. Everyone had been so happy and kindly in the way that they had reacted, in wishing them a happy married life and repeatedly conveying how deeply they cared about them. It had been as if part of their own elation had spread to everybody else and they had all felt part of a unified whole and equally happy. She and Cecil had risen to the occasion, but so had everyone else.

She can still see Daddy and Cecil's father sitting beside each other, after the meal was over, having what Cecil's father, Pop Connolly, had always called a "good chin-wag". They had been enveloped in an absolute smog of tobacco smoke, Daddy with his pipe and Pop with his tenth Woodbine of the day. She had gone over to them and sat with them for a while, she remembers. Their conversation had been all about the roads of County Carlow and County Wicklow, where they had been as young men and what they had seen and done. They had been born and brought up only ten miles from each other, Pop in Bagenalstown and Daddy in Baltinglass, and so had known many people in common in their younger years. Noreen, in looking back, wonders at how well they had managed to get along, really well considering that her Daddy had been such a strong Irish nationalist and Pop had served in the British Army and sometimes spoke like an Irishman speaking with an English accent. And her Mummy and Cecil's had been absolute angels, no other word for it. They had worked tirelessly all day, making sure that everybody had felt welcomed, had got their cake and champagne on time, and cups of tea whenever they wanted them; whilst she and Cecil had been left free to circulate and be gracious and entertaining for their guests.

When they had got back from Westminster Cathedral, Cecil had busied himself ringing Knights of Saint Columba contacts based in London, from the hotel room. Later he had announced that he was going to a meeting with the local Grand Knight in Holland Park. Noreen had been left with little option but to explore the room's facil-ities on her own and had been impressed to find that the hotel provided headed notepaper and envelopes for the use of guests.

Once Cecil had left, Noreen had immediately settled herself at the pretty rosewood and walnut writing table which was beside the window overlooking the Strand, to write to her parents. The headed notepaper was distinctive, green print with a green border and a hotel crest at the top, with a telephone number and telegram address provided just beneath the crest. To her consternation, Noreen noticed the hotel boasted thirty one telephone lines, significantly reducing any prospect that Cecil would be reining in his use of the telephone. However she had been determined to write home and had dutifully composed a chatty letter describing the décor in their room, the view from their window, the falling sleet and the heavy clouds which were threatening but not producing heavy snowfalls. The rest of the morning passed slowly for Noreen, she remembers, until Cecil had arrived back breathless, just in time for luncheon. The menu had been in French which had suited Noreen down to the ground – Saumon à la Mayonnaise, Aloyau de Boeuf Rôti, Hanche d'Agneau, Jambon à l'Anglaise, Langue de Boeuf à la Gelée, Salade à la Jardinière, Pommes-de-Terre au Beurre, Macédoine aux Fruits, Chantilly Trifle, Tarte aux Prunes, Glace à la Vanille, Fromage, and Biscuits. Cecil had been disgusted it was not in English, but had eaten well nonetheless.

Over lunch Cecil had confided in Noreen that the Knights of Saint Columba had hopes of securing a property in Holland Park, to turn it into a Residential Club which Knights from all around the country could use. The wine waiter had recommended claret, which they had sipped conspiratorially. Cecil had never before told Noreen anything about the Knights' business, and, when the claret was finished, they had decided to spend a relaxing afternoon together, and had retired to their room for the rest of the day.

The highlight of the next day was a visit to a concert given by the tenor, John McCormack, at the Streatham Hill Palace. McCormack had been in the twilight of his singing days. He had retired once and then started performing again to help the Red Cross and the war effort. But the songs had been romantic and touching, 'The Garden where the Praties Grow', 'Oft in the Stilly Night' and 'The Green Isle of Erin'. Noreen had found herself humming the tunes softly to herself, for the rest of their honeymoon.

"We had a nice time in the Strand Palace Hotel, didn't we? It was a good choice?"

Cecil nods. "A very good choice."

Noreen puts the box of souvenirs back into Cecil's locker.

"By the way, it's tomorrow I've booked us into The Copthorne for lunch, to celebrate our anniversary."

Cecil's face clouds over.

"No, I can't go there... I haven't been out of *this* hotel properly yet..."

"Don't worry sweet. You won't have to do anything. I've got it all arranged."

May, 1999

CECIL has woken once today already. Has eaten a good breakfast. And then slept again. Now, he is up on one elbow, leaning out of his bed. Stretching his hand haphazardly towards his locker. Urgently searching for something. His gavel. He is sure there is a meeting at the KSC Club in Canton later on. He needs to get the agenda typed up too. The gavel is not there – nor his typewriter. But he notices his box of souvenirs. Safely locked and tucked away under some books. Its key, he knows, is resting safely in his wallet. The letters inside already read and relished for one year. Something to look forward to next year, he thinks. Next February. When we will have been married... a long, long time.

Pity we did not make it to The Cupthorne, or Copthorne, whatever it was called. For that lunch. Cecil rolls himself back into the centre of his bed. Was just a touch bilious on the morning of the big day, he remembers. Noreen had worried he might catch a chill. Pity. She had so wanted him to be able to go. And he had wanted to take her. Could have got all dressed up, like we used to. Maybe next year.

The effort of searching in his locker has tired him. Cecil turns onto his right side. His laboured breathing becomes more settled. He is warm and comfortable. Sometimes he is in a deep slumber. In between, he keeps coming to with a sudden start, "Must have drowsed off... Ye'm. That'll be it..."

Cecil is hot now. Restless. His skin is itching. Like it itched when he wore his uniform. They had not let him into the Army. That had been hard. His eyesight was always very poor. And he had never been physically co-ordinated, he knew. That was why he hated ball-games so much. And he had always been thin. You can count every rib, Mammy had always said. Physically substandard or something equally hurtful, the medical board had said. But the Local Defence Volunteers in Frome had welcomed him with open arms. Had given him a thick prickly uniform which he had worn proudly, although it was so uncomfortable. Dad's Army they call us now. But they wouldn't have laughed if ever we had been needed. We were ready to do our bit... To pay the final price, if called to do so.

It had been work at the office during the day time, Home Guard in the evenings, and fire-watching at weekends in London during the Blitz. There had hardly been time to think. I was one of the lucky ones though, Cecil reflects. Able to go home to Noreen at the end of most days. Not spending half my life cooped up in a plane, or a tank, or a submarine, waiting to be blown to smithereens by a shell or a depth charge. He tries to stretch his legs out fully but they are weak and, annoyingly, his big toe gets caught in a fold in his lower sheet.

Noreen had not been so lucky though. Losing their baby. Little Philomena. Cecil's only daughter. Cecil stares wide-eyed at the edge of his pillow. 1941 or '42, it had been. He can still picture the shrivelled little face, swathed all about in a towelling bandage, lying in the side ward, where they left her for a few hours after the birth. Cecil strives to free his big toe from the sheet. His toenail catches in the fabric. He lies still. May she rest in peace. Little Philomena. Their joy over Sean's arrival had been all the greater, Cecil thinks. A bouncing baby boy. But they had to wait some years for him. When eventually he did arrive, they saw him as a gift from God. Truly, a gift from God.

Time had flown by. They had moved to Cardiff when Cecil got promotion.

A mist descends over Cecil's eyes and he watches it spread more widely across the silver surface of Dozmary Pool. He is dressed in heavy armour and riding a fine white steed along the shore. His feet held firm in his stirrups. His journey has been long, but he has a sense that this fine lake is his destination. Through the slits in the visor of his helmet, he spies a damsel. Long dark hair draped over her shoulders, far down her back. She is clad in fine white chiffon which embraces her limbs and swirls out behind as if there is a breeze blowing, though Cecil is perspiring freely inside his suit of armour. Ethereal is the word, Cecil thinks. The only word, for this vision of delight. The maiden is not in distress as he had first thought. Her step is light, even coquettish. As he gallops up, she half turns and smiles up at him. He bends low from the waist and sweeps her up and onto his horse to sit behind him. They do not speak; they just laugh conspiratorially about their pact, made so instinctively. The horse's hooves pound on. It is taking them away from the pool. To his castle, he assumes. He has no idea of the way. The mist thickens, causing droplets of moisture to form on the horse's mane. For no apparent reason, he has a belief that the horse is on course, that they will arrive.

Cecil's mouth is dry. His tongue feels swollen. He smiles bitterly to himself. The drought had started when his parents moved in. After he and Noreen had bought the house in Cardiff. Noreen had found it hard. Not having privacy. Had joined the drama group, to get out of the house in the evenings. That was what caused her to go off the rails. All those kitchen sink dramas. 'Look Back In Anger' and 'The Birthday Party'. Osbourne, Pinter. All those so-called intellectuals stirring people up.

What was he called, that fellow Noreen played with in 'The Birthday Party', Cecil asks himself? A brute of a man, he was. Steel-erector in the daytime. The biggest Steel-erector in Cardiff, I shouldn't wonder. There was Noreen up on stage playing his landlady, touching his big bare arms, fluttering her eyelids at him and and talking suggestively about whether his corn flakes were nice and succulent. Disgusting. Cecil recalls going back stage to congratulate Noreen on her performance, even though he had hated the play. He could swear they had been up to something. In the corridor outside the dressing room. They had moved apart too quickly when he had come through the stage door. Noreen had been quick to recover. Ever the actress. But he had felt certain that she was simultaneously tucking in some of her clothing with her free hand, as she encircled the back of his neck with the other. Cecil had been too surprised to say anything. Had in any case not been sure of what he had seen.

Then there had been Othello, in which Noreen had played the part of Desdemona. Cecil had thought Shakespeare would be alright. More traditional. Breeding a sense of propriety within the cast members. But, oh no! Cecil had become convinced that he had detected traces of Othello's black make-up on Noreen's brassière, on several occasions.

Then there had been her brief encounter with Dr Faustus, whom she had directed in an extremely well received production of the play. Cecil had begun to fear that Noreen would be risking her own immortal soul with her behaviour, if she continued with her antics as he called them. Though he never had any proof that his concerns were valid, he had been convinced that the rehearsals were unnecessarily long. Why did she choose to do a play where the rehearsals would effectively involve only one other person for hours on end? And why did she cast Othello as Dr Faustus?

He could not get these questions out of his mind. And, he recalls, he was only concerned about it because he loved her so much. But it had not helped. Telling Noreen of his suspicions. She had threatened to jump out of the car. The old Ford Popular it had been. They were driving up to Rhosllanerchrugog at the time, to visit Noreen's parents. "*What?...*" Noreen had said. "*What?...*" And she had half opened the door on her side of the car. He had been driving at 55 miles per hour. He knows the speed he was doing because he remembers looking at the speedometer and thinking she could be killed if she jumps out now. He slowed the car, but did not stop completely. After a long and stony silence between them, he had said, "Shall we leave it there then?" Noreen had nodded. Cecil can still see the expression on Noreen's face. Enigmatic is how I would describe it, Cecil murmurs pensively. Yes, enigmatic. The subject was closed – never to be broached by either again.

Both continued to labour hard at their respective interests, Noreen with her dramatic roles and productions and the Catholic Marriage Advisory Council; Cecil with the Knights of Saint Columba and The Civil Service Catholic Guild. The number of downstairs rooms, in their comfortable house on Marlborough Hill, meant that Cecil could type at will and hold as many meetings as he liked – in the dining room, and Noreen could learn her lines and have a steady stream of callers – in the lounge; whilst Sean and Cecil's parents, and later Noreen's mother, had ample space in their rooms upstairs or in the breakfast room downstairs.

NOREEN DRIVES SLOWLY down Marlborough Hill. She stays in second gear until she reaches the bottom of the slope and then carefully turns left into Romilly Road. The Corsa is just right for her. Small and manoeuvrable, though the steering is a bit heavy. She has rushed her breakfast to get out this morning. That is the way it goes. Sometimes she is up with the lark. Sometimes she has to push herself a bit. It is quite different without Cecil at home. When Cecil was at home, she muses, he was always up at seven and cooking the bacon by 7.15. Sometimes, she does not wake up until 8.30 these days. Still, they have a lot to be grateful for. Cecil is so near.

Noreen squashes between two badly-parked vehicles in the car park. She opens her car door as far as she can and with difficulty manages to extricate herself from her car. She pushes hard through the very firm swing doors and then stops for a chat with the receptionist. She has got to know her quite well over the months.

When Noreen reaches Cecil's room, she finds him fast asleep. She need not have rushed. Still, she is there. And will be there when Cecil wakes, all being well.

Noreen looks through the window at her favourite view, towards Penarth Head. It is clearer than she had thought. Driving down, she had not noticed what the weather was doing. The sun is actually shining quite strongly over Penarth. And there are seagulls flying inland. Sometimes that means it is going to rain, she thinks.

She notices Cecil has run out of water and uses the jug on his locker to pour some out for him.

She leafs through a copy of the *Western Mail.* Cecil must have ordered it. She scans through the Births,

Marriages and Deaths. Nobody she knows today. It is warm in the room. She is aware of herself sitting motionless. Waiting for Cecil to wake. She could go and sit on the landing by the big window, where a group of staff and residents are always seated. It would be company. But she would not have a lot to say to them. She feels a heaviness in her limbs. She decides to wait.

She gazes at the crucifix on Cecil's wall.

One of the Nuns pops in to say hello. Sister Roberta. Spends a few minutes whispering loudly with Noreen about how well Cecil is doing. How he has been talking to them all a bit more.

"I think he's getting used to us now, Mrs Connolly!"

"Oh, yes, Sister. I think he's very happy here..."

The Nun goes on her way.

The tea-trolley arrives and then continues on its travels again, after Noreen has been given a cup of tea.

Noreen says a few prayers of thanksgiving. They have both been so well through most of their retirement. Their son, Sean, settled with his wife in Caerphilly. Cecil has the problem with his legs now, but he copes. And they have both been lucky with all the kindly recognition they have received from other people. Noreen being made a life member of the drama group. And both of them being given a Papal Award for their work for the Church. Noreen with the Catholic Marriage Advisory Service and Cecil with the Knights of Saint Columba and the Civil Service Guild. *Pro Ecclesia Et Pontifice*. Cecil had tried to be modest about it, but inside he had been like a man who has just won an Olympic Medal, she is sure. The icing on the cake had been when Cecil had been selected to meet the Pope in person, during the Pope's visit to Cardiff in 1982. Cecil's favourite hymn had always been, 'God bless The Pope', and now he would meet him in person. God's representative on earth.

It had almost seemed as if there was nothing more they could achieve, from a spiritual point of view. But, it is how we live our lives that counts, not any honours which we may be fortunate enough to receive, Cecil had said sternly, and Noreen had agreed. It was people that counted.

Cecil wakes with a start. He looks at Noreen.

"Oh... You!"

"Yes... It's me, Cecil. Are you pleased?"

"I've been dreaming..."

"Yes, but are you pleased to see me?"

"Ye'm... of course I am..."

"I should think so, too! I've been sitting here for ages."

"Have you?"

"Yes, ages and ages... So what were you dreaming about?"

"Oh... just a woman who comes in here sometimes..."

"I'm going to have to watch you... you're a dark horse, even if the Pope did give you one of his *Pro Ecclesia Et Pontifice* Decorations... He doesn't know you, does he?!"

৪৩

NOREEN is getting ready for bed. Thank God, she sleeps well. She always has done, apart from when she was pregnant with Sean.

She slips into her nightie. The room is not overlooked and is sufficiently long for her to change in total privacy, so long as she stands well back. She does not lower the Venetian blinds or draw the curtains anymore. Cecil used to lower the Venetian blinds with a clatter every night, and draw the curtains, before they switched the light off. Noreen leaves them open. There is a street-light outside, half-obscured by the tree. She likes the half-light it gives off to shine into her room.

In the summer, when she lies in bed and looks out through the bay window, she can see the tree's luxuriantly clad boughs and she imagines herself in a cosy nest with the birds. Spring is here, she thinks, smiling at the leaves which have already come, bright green but flecked with orange light. She sleeps.

Noreen wakes with a yawn. She stretches. Visits the bathroom. Returns to the bedroom to get dressed. Something in tweed, she thinks, and explores her wardrobe. She finds a tweed suit with a smart, classic cut and turned back cuffs. She chooses brown shoes to go with the green suit.

"Comfortable shoes are so important," she mutters to herself. Leather is essential for her feet now. To let them breathe. Can't beat A.G. Meek's, she thinks. She sits to lever her shoes on with a shoe-horn. She sits up and pauses to catch her breath.

Sometimes, she remembers how her bedroom was when she and Cecil gave it up so that Cecil's parents could use it. She pictures Pop Connolly. Remembers how she used to find him sitting there in the window, when she took up his cup of tea after dinner. Watching the cars going up and down Marlborough Hill, sometimes late into the evening. Shading his eyes against the evening sun with both hands, like a captain on the bridge of a ship, looking for land.

She had been run off her feet, she remembers, in those days. Never had any time to look out of a window herself. What with her teaching, and all the cooking, washing, and cleaning she had to do. Minnie had been a God-send. Pure gold. But they had only employed her for four hours a day. Minnie had not been able to do everything. What Minnie had not had time to do, Noreen had needed to do. And bringing up a son more or less single-handedly. Cecil had been so busy. Doing things for and with other people. He had always wanted her to be involved in the social side of things, of course, but Noreen had felt that to be an intrusion into her time, when there was so much else she was trying to do.

She sometimes feels a stab of resentment, that her time was so taken up. She feels she could have achieved so much more with her life.

Still, she tells herself, she could have done worse. She has a lot to be grateful for. Cecil has been faithful, and dependable. Through it all. She does sometimes wonder what her life would have been like, if she had married Eric. Still, she will settle for Cecil. Yes. She could have done worse.

℘

NOREEN WAKES WITH A START. Another day. Wait. She can hear the telephone ringing. A quarter to eight. Who can be ringing her at this hour?

"Mrs Connolly?"

"Yes..."

"Sister Roberta, Mrs Connolly. I don't want to frighten you, but I think you should come down."

"It's Cecil isn't it?"

"He may not have long, Mrs Connolly. I'm sorry."

Noreen drives furiously down Marlborough Hill, a feeling of panic invading her stomach.

"Please, God. Let him last."

Noreen is in Cecil's room. Sister Roberta has been sitting with him. She explains the Doctor has already been to see Cecil, about six o'clock that morning. He had said that there was nothing to be done. Cecil was comfortable. The temperature he had been suffering from had turned into pneumonia, and at his age, it could be hours or a few more days. But Sister Roberta had felt it might be sooner rather than later and had decided to ring Noreen. She had rung Sean too, in Caerphilly. He had already left for work but his wife had agreed to let him know. The priest had just finished giving Cecil the Last Rites, before Noreen arrived. They had turned Cecil onto his side, so he was able to see into the room.

"I'll leave you together, Mrs Connolly."

Noreen stands beside Cecil. He seems hot. Feverish. She takes his hand.

"Cecil?"

Cecil does not answer. His breathing is extremely laboured. But Noreen can see from his eyes that he can hear her. She draws up a chair beside the bed. She talks gently to Cecil about anything and everything. Reassures him.

Cecil feels very tired. He is concentrating on his breathing. He can see Noreen is there. He is glad she is there. Good old thing. Less of the 'old', she would say, if she had known what he was thinking. There is a slight haze around her head, but he can see her eyes alright. They are fixed on him. She is talking to him. He likes the sound of her voice. She speaks so clearly but gently at the same time. Cecil is afraid because he feels out of control. Now Noreen is here, he hopes things will settle down. He feels a bit calmer. The Doctor had not seemed to have much to say. A young chap. Never met him before. At least, Cecil does not remember meeting him before. A new wave of fear comes over Cecil. He thinks to himself they must think it's serious. Sending for the priest.

"Are you in any pain, darling?"

Noreen squeezes Cecil's hand gently.

He gives the merest shake of his head.

Noreen experiences a slight sense of relief, but she feels the world should be standing still. Nothing else has any importance, at this moment. Yet, she is frighteningly aware of time rushing forward.

Cecil takes an extra-large, laboured breath. He is looking at Noreen. Does not take his eyes off her. His look. Everything is telescoped into that expression in his eyes. Helplessness, desperate hope.

Cecil's breathing stops. Noreen sees the life literally leave his eyes. Those eyes she has looked into, on and off, for 59 years. Ever since she first looked into them in the Church in Chard. And she saw that softness, helplessness, which she could not resist.

Noreen spends a minute sitting with Cecil, then goes to find Sister Roberta.

Sister Roberta comes. And a few other nuns, who begin prayers for the dead. They are doing it to help Noreen. To give her comfort. She is grateful. But the main comfort she feels is that she arrived in time. To be with Cecil, when the time came. She has a sense that he was glad that she was there to hold his hand on the edge of the abyss, and to look eternity in the eye. And she is grateful that he has gone first. She does not know how he would have coped without her.

Noreen is aware of Sean arriving, about fifteen minutes later. She watches him go in to say farewell to Cecil. When he comes out of Cecil's room, Noreen has no desire to stay. She drives up to Marlborough Hill. Puts the kettle on. Drinks a cup of tea with Sean. He tells her he will take care of some practical tasks. Ringing the undertaker. Registering Cecil's death. Putting an announcement in the *Western Mail*.

At the funeral, Noreen greets everybody effusively. Thanks them. So many people. So kind of them, she thinks.

After the funeral, there is a gathering in Churchill's Hotel. Overlooking Llandaff Fields. Plates of sandwiches. More cups of tea. Noreen cannot get over the number of people who attend. Cecil would really have appreciated it, she thinks. Such a good turn-out.

❦

NINE MONTHS have passed, since Cecil died. Noreen sees that the letter lying on the front doormat has a Worcester post code. She assumes it is from Digby.

Digby had been married to Margaret, Noreen's friend from her Convent days.

Noreen had not been in touch with Margaret for years and years. Then they had met up by chance at an event in London for regional organisers of The Catholic Marriage Advisory Council and had kept in frequent contact after that. Noreen had visited Margaret and Digby's home and she had written regularly, so that Margaret had become one of Noreen's closest friends again. Then Margaret had died, after a short illness. Poor Digby had been devastated. Noreen had done her best to console him and spent hours on the phone listening, as he gradually came to terms with his loss.

With Cecil gone, Digby was returning the huge kindness Noreen had shown him in his hour of need. His last letter had urged Noreen to come up to stay for a week. To enjoy a change of scene, and let him spoil her for a while. Noreen had not really felt ready for such a trip, and had made her excuses. Apart from anything else, Digby's house brought back such sad memories. It had been where she had spent many happy hours with Margaret, and where all four of them had enjoyed each other's company.

Noreen picks the letter up from the doormat, along with a cluster of junk mail. The letter is even more persuasive than the last.

Dear Noreen,

How are you? Well, I hope. I am fine. Not a lot I can do in the garden at this time of year, but I have been spending a few weekends down at my daughter's house in Cheltenham. It makes a nice change, and it's delightful to be with the grandchildren for however short a time.

When I was at my daughter's last weekend, I made a firm resolution – that I would ask you up here for a few days, but, rather than just visit me without any particular purpose, I will arrange for us to go to a Shakespeare play at Stratford-on-Avon, performed by the Royal Shakespeare Company. Now, Noreen, I happen to know that you love Shakespeare and that you particularly like seeing him performed at Stratford, so no excuses this time – we are going!

Shall give you a ring next Tuesday evening to tell you the time of the train you need to catch. I'll be at the station on Wednesday to collect you at the appointed time.

Your good friend,
Digby.

Noreen tucks the letter behind the clock. She loves going to Stratford, but she has misgivings. She cannot imagine watching 'Romeo and Juliet', with Digby. It would be just too embarrassing. And, if it turned out to be 'A Winter's Tale', it would be so depressing.

The play itself is fine. 'A Midsummer Night's Dream'. They have a meal afterwards, looking out over the Avon. Digby is so considerate. Noreen cannot help but be moved. But, nonetheless, she asks him to drive her to the station a day early, to catch the return train. She simply cannot settle away from her own home.

As Noreen walks along the platform at Cardiff Station, she sees Sean is already there to meet her.

"You're limping, Mum."

"I think I must have pulled a muscle or something, in my side. It's nothing."

Noreen decides she will take things a bit more easily, in future. Racketing about at her age is not a good idea.

Noreen had visited Cecil twice a day for so long. When he had died in the May, it had left her with a lot of time on her hands. She had been used to a routine. And she had enjoyed going to Mass every day.

She could no longer visit Cecil, but she realised there was no reason why she could not continue going to Mass every day. She reverted to attending Mass at Saint Mary of The Angels, her normal parish. She saw the same people there, most of whom she had known for years, and it gave shape to her day.

She knew Cecil would have wanted her to soldier on. Not give up. And she did that to the best of her ability.

If she is honest, she thinks, there were times when she had found it hard, at the beginning. She had felt strangely detached at times. Like the day she parked her car before morning Mass, and then, when Mass was over, had spent three quarters of an hour walking around Canton, trying to remember where she had parked it. And there had been those other times, when she could not help going up to Omar's shop, convinced she needed foodstuffs and sauces with which to cook a Sunday lunch for herself and Cecil. If she really faces facts, although she was keeping herself busy, she had not really felt anything mattered very much any more. Without Cecil around with whom she could share the events of the day, life had lacked an essential dimension.

But everybody had told her, it takes time. And, indeed, as the weeks and months had passed by, she had noticed glimmerings of normality coming back. She had begun to think that perhaps it really would make sense to move Cecil's things out of the bedroom. But she had not done so. She had a fear that if she moved his things out, the floodgates could open and she might lose her self-control, which she felt she could not allow to happen now that she was alone.

Finally, motivated by an accumulation of fine dust on Cecil's side of the bedroom, Noreen had decided to make a start by at least tidying Cecil's things. She would not throw anything out yet, she thought, just keep everything clean and tidy for the time being. His wardrobe. There was quite a clutter of things piled up at the bottom of it. Old shoes. The trousers of his dinner suit, still spick and span in their trouser press. Beach sandals which he had not worn for years. Then, to her surprise, underneath an old brown dressing gown which had slipped off its hanger, Noreen came across her beloved writing case. The one Cecil had given her when she was teaching in the convent in Chard. Its original, pristine blue leather was faded, and no handle graced its upper edge, but the usual thrill of anticipation still went through Noreen as she placed the case carefully on the bed. How it had found its way to the bottom of Cecil's wardrobe she had no idea. Cecil hated throwing things away. Perhaps he had salvaged it during one of her periodic clear outs. She smiled, remembering the struggle she used to have even to get Cecil to throw out last week's newspapers.

Inside the case, still in its envelope, Noreen found a letter Cecil had written to her. Her legs began to feel weak and she sat down on the bed to read it. It had been written just before their wedding.

My Darling Noreen

I pray that this will be the last time that I shall address an envelope to you in the same way as the one containing this letter is addressed. Also, that it will be but rarely that it is necessary to write to you, since I hope that we may not often be separated. If it be possible, I want to spend the rest of my life with you.

All goes well with the house, by the way. Lots of food in, in case we need it.

In a matter of days, please God, we shall each be turning over a new page in the stories of our individual lives, but we shall equally, I think, as far as all that is "ours" is concerned, be commencing life anew. An amazing prospect!

I hope that I may be able to use this opportunity to the full. I want to try to become a little more worthy of you, you who have consented to give to me all that you have to give. Please pray that so priceless a gift will inspire me with an increased love for you, which will never cease to increase.

Noreen noticed that Cecil had been interrupted at this point, or had perhaps run out of inspiration, as the letter breaks off there without explanation. It recommences the next day, by which time Cecil has received a letter from Noreen.

Wed. 21st Feb. 1940

Thank you for your letter. Please find enclosed the list you asked for, concerning the wedding cake boxes, etc. Could discussion of the other bits and bobs you mention wait until we meet? It would be handy, though, if you would check soonest that they do have rooms available at the

Carlton Hotel. Spending the night before my wedding day with my parents in an Austin Seven is not an attractive prospect I am afraid, much though I love them!

Oh, yes. The presents. Provided they are not too bulky, I think it will be best to bring them with us, so we should return to Frome first, I think, before travelling on to London.

It is still bitterly cold down here. However, nil desperandum, the parents and I hope to make the journey on Sunday or Monday. It is probable that we shall arrive about dusk, when we will make for your house. Do not become alarmed, my love, if we should be late.

I now wish you good night, and may God bless you, and may he grant us the grace to enable us to live lives worthy of each other from now on.

All my love
Cecil.

Noreen carefully replaced the letter in its envelope and the envelope back in the case. Unsure where she should keep it, she returned the case to the wardrobe.

She got up off the bed. She had a lot to be thankful for, she reminded herself. There was still plenty to do, but she would leave tidying for today. She would set about preparing some tea now.

ANOTHER TWO MONTHS have passed. Noreen knows she is dying and is fully reconciled to the fact. She has been in Hospital for three weeks, and is now at home. The doctors at the hospital reached a diagnosis without exploratory operations. Noreen is grateful for this, but she feels she has been away for a long time. Her joy at being back in her own home knows no bounds.

Some people would say there is no hope, but Noreen does not see it in terms of hope or otherwise. She accepts.

Noreen is in the front lounge, on a single bed, for ease of access by the medical support staff. Every flower imaginable, and dozens of Good Wishes cards, adorn the mantlepiece. Many visitors have called during the last two days and, every time, she has risen to the occasion to make her visitor feel welcome. She appreciates them so much.

Noreen is no longer eating or drinking and is swiftly getting weaker. Her neighbours from Bangladesh are standing on the pavement outside in beautiful colourful robes, a sign of respect for the dying, having paid their last respects in person; the priest comes and tells Noreen there is nothing he needs to absolve her of, she has led a good life. Noreen smiles and thanks him in a whisper. She is finding it hard to talk.

Sean and his wife have been sitting with Noreen through the last nights. She has been uncomfortable but not in pain. Today the nurses have given her morphine-based medicine for the first time. Just a few drops have helped Noreen to relax a little more.

Every so often, she asks if Sean or his wife are there. They speak to her. Then start singing. Noreen joins in as well as she can. Simple songs. Children's nursery rhymes which Noreen sang to Sean as a child. Sean encourages her to sing. Praises her efforts. Knowing how she values being able to express herself. Noreen relishes the activity. She laughs with pleasure when she does well. She is lalala-ing to Brahms' Lullaby, when she grows tired. She looks up, as if she is able to see someone. Her mother, standing with her hand on Cecil's shoulder. Her father on the other side. They are smiling at her, beckoning her forward. Noreen stops singing, sinks into a deep slumber, before dying, a few seconds later.

IT IS the second anniversary of Cecil's death. Thirteen months since Noreen died. An evening in May. That quiet time, before dusk falls. The house where Noreen and Cecil lived on Marlborough Hill has been sold. From deep inside the house nextdoor comes the faintest clatter and clink of plates, knives and forks, and aromas of food cooking – a hint of cardamom in the air, coriander, dill, clove, ginger, bay, fennel, cumin. In the school grounds across the road, fragrant wisps from a bonfire drift like incense through the green boughs of the trees facing the house.

In Chard, where their story began, the small grey church, where Cecil and Noreen met, still stands. Grey stone, with the priest's presbytery next door. But the garden has gone. The site of the convent, demolished many years previously, now lies beneath a busy road. Gone the orchard, the laurel bushes, Judy the cow, the fields, and most of the thick green trees. Modern bungalows and side roads cover the land where the convent grounds once extended. The remaining trees mark the remnants of the old boundary. Their profiles sharp against a lovely evening sky.

Acknowledgments

Thanks to my brother, Chris Corcoran, for permission to use letters written by our mother, Norah Corcoran, as the basis for the letters which appear in this novel. Thanks also to Eleanor, his wife; my sister-in-law, Josephine Smullen, and her husband, James, for reading through the original typescript; to Will Atkins for his editorship; and to Ann, my wife, for her encouragement and support.

The Author

Patrick Corcoran lives in Tonteg, south Wales. He works for the Children and Family Court Advisory and Support Service. His first novel, *Last Light Breaking*, was published by Seren in 1998.